Tiger by the Tail

Tiger by the Tail

Eric Walters

An imprint of
Beach Holme Publishing
Vancouver, B.C.

This book is published by Beach Holme Publishing, #226—2040 West 12th Ave., Vancouver, BC, V6J 2G2. This is a Sandcastle Book.

The publisher and author acknowledge the generous assistance of The Canada Council and the BC Ministry of Small Business, Tourism and Culture.

THE CANADA COUNCIL FOR THE ARTS SINCE 1957 | LE CONSEIL DES ARTS DU CANADA DEPUIS 1957

Editor: Joy Gugeler
Cover Illustration: Ron Lightburn
Production and Design: Teresa Bubela

Canadian Cataloguing in Publication Data

Walters, Eric, 1957-
  Tiger by the tail

(A Sandcastle Book)
ISBN 0-88878-396-5

  I. Title.
PS8595.A598T53 1999   jC813'.54   C99-910309-1
PZ7.W17129Ti 1999

To Mary, Walter and Russ:

three people who not only have
tigers by the tail
but also in their hearts.

Chapter 1

"Nicholas do you have *any idea* where you're going?" I asked.

"Of course I do, Sarah. I'm going *this* way," he answered as he ducked down and disappeared under the fence.

The fence was high, way above my head, solid wood, peeling paint, topped off with a few strands of rusty barbed wire. I bent down, turned sideways and eased my head and shoulders under the fence. My brother was walking away.

"Nicholas! Come back here, we just can't walk through somebody's property!"

He turned to face me. "Look around. Do you think anybody cares if we walk through here?"

He did have a point. He was standing in what looked like an abandoned field. Instead of crops there were scattered weeds poking out of the rutted and sun-baked soil. Nobody had farmed this land for a while.

"Still, we shouldn't be cutting across somebody else's property. Let's just go back and go home along the road," I suggested.

"Sarah you're my older sister...not my mother. Our house

is *that* way," he said pointing in the direction he had been walking. "And if we don't take this short cut that storm is going to get to us before we get to our house."

Storm clouds were racing in from the east; winds were picking up, the air was suddenly cooler and we could see lightning and hear thunder in the distance.

I didn't want to follow him, but I didn't want to get soaked in the storm. "I guess we have to go your way."

"Good, maybe we can get home before we get wet."

"Wet isn't what I'm worried about, Nicholas."

"It's July, Sarah, so I don't think it's going to snow," Nicholas said in his snarkiest voice. He had a smart aleck answer for everything.

"I'm worried about...tornados," I practically whispered.

"Tornados!"

"Be quiet!" I scolded.

"Be quiet? Why, do you think if you say it too loud one will show up?" Nicholas laughed.

"Yes...I mean no. I mean...just be quiet. You know this is tornado country."

"Since when?"

"Two weeks ago a tornado touched down just a few miles from here."

"It did?" Nicholas said.

"Yes. It damaged some crops and overturned a hay wagon."

"Are you sure about that?"

"Of course I am. I read it in the paper."

I looked up even more anxiously at the sky. While we'd been talking the sky had darkened and the wind had picked up. I scanned the horizon for funnel clouds.

"Get going and I'll follow," I said.

Nicholas started off and I trailed behind him.

"Do you really know where you're going?" I questioned.

"Of course. I'm walking through an abandoned field."

"But..."

"Don't worry, sis, it's all under control."

The wind was now so strong it was pushing us along. Little pieces of dried up stalk and leaves and dirt hurled through the air as we moved. It was getting darker. There was a flash of lightning, so bright that it lit up the sky, followed almost instantly by a clap of thunder.

I remembered from science class that if a burst of lightning and the sound of the thunder are that close together a storm is almost on top of you. Another jagged strip of lightning flashed and in that second I caught sight of Nick's face. He looked as scared as I felt. I braced for another explosion of thunder then the first few drops of rain began to fall.

"We're not going to make it," Nicholas said. He couldn't even pretend to be brave now.

"Let's move it."

Nicholas started sprinting and then stopped suddenly, turning to face me. "Sarah, I can't remember, is it better to have on rubber-soled shoes or not?"

"What? What are you talking about?"

"The lightning, the lightning! I remember reading that it won't hit you if you have rubber on the bottom of your shoes ...or was it that if you had rubber on the bottom of your shoes you *would* get hit? I can't remember!"

"I don't know," I answered, trying to remain calm in the face of his panic.

More flashes of lightning, immediately followed by the crashes of thunder.

"Maybe we should...," my mind raced ahead for an answer, "...maybe we should take off one of our shoes. Then at least we'll be safe half the time." As I said this I realized it was a ridiculous suggestion, but Nicholas was so scared he didn't even question me. He bent down and took off his left running shoe. I did the same with my left sandal.

"We're not going to make it home," I said. "Maybe we can find some shelter. Come on!"

Nicholas fell in behind me. We raced across the bumps and ridges of the open field. The crusty ground was becoming damp and soft and I knew that once the rain really came down this whole field would be mud. At that instant the rain started to come down in earnest. We ran even harder, but within steps I was soaked and my clothes clung to my body. A flash of lightning seared the sky above us.

"Look!" Nicholas screamed. "Up ahead!"

Through the heavy rain and the darkness I could make out the outline of what looked like a barn. We headed straight for it. We stumbled out of the field and onto a gravel driveway. It led straight up to the building. It was good not to be running in the mud anymore but the stones hurt my one bare foot.

"Don't slow down!" Nicholas screamed as he raced past me, then stopped right in front of the old barn. It towered over us; two stories high, weathered old grey boards, vines growing up the sides and a large door, closed.

"Let's get inside!" he hollered over the noise the rain was making as it pounded against the barn's tin roof.

"We can't just go inside, it doesn't belong to us!"

"Give me a break! I'm going inside. You can stand out here until you get hit by lightning for all I care!" he screamed..

I stood there watching. Nicholas pushed against the door. It wouldn't open. He moved first to one side and then the other. He found a smaller door and disappeared from view.

"Nicholas!" I ran after him to discover Nicholas calmly sitting inside the barn on a bale of hay.

"We shouldn't be here without permission," I reminded him, trying my best to imitate mom.

"Yeah, Sarah, right. Who do you think we're going to get permission from? A ghost? Besides, I've got a bigger problem."

"What?" I asked with concern.

"My sock. Somewhere out there the mud sucked it off my foot." He held up his bare, muddy, size seven.

"That's your problem?" I asked in disbelief.

"Yeah. Mom said that the next time I lost anything she'd make me pay. I've got better things to do with my allowance than buy socks."

I sat down on a bale of hay myself and put my sandal on. The other sandal was unrecognizable underneath a layer of mud.

"I hope this storm stops soon. We don't want anybody to come along and find us," I said.

"Find us? Look around. There hasn't been anybody in here for a long time."

I let my eyes scan the building. There were so many missing boards that the gaps between the boards let the light stream in from the outside. But those same gaps let in more than just light. I could also feel a steady spray from the rain. It was drier, but not dry.

Over in one corner there was some broken-down, old machinery. Hanging up on one wall were three old, rusty bikes. Right beside us was a pile of old tires and a worn out couch, partially covered in plastic. Beams criss-crossed the roof, and all sorts of ropes hung down.

The floor was covered with a thin layer of dirty straw and there were a few bales of hay off to one side. The noise of the rain hitting the tin roof was punctuated by the sound of boards, only partially attached, clapping in the wind.

I stood up. "Nicholas, what do you think...." As I turned around I realized he wasn't where he'd been sitting. He'd wandered off while I was busy peering around the barn.

"Nicholas..." I called out hesitantly. There was no answer.

"Nick..." I called again, this time louder. There was no reply, only the steady drumming of the rain which seemed to be getting louder. I stood up and took a few steps, but stopped as my muddy sandal thickened with a layer of straw and mud on its sole.

"Oh, great," I muttered. I tried to wipe it off against the floor. Instead, more straw became attached. It looked like a welcome mat that was stuck to the bottom of my foot. I leaned against a beam, rubbing the bottom of my sandal until most of the mud and straw plopped to the floor.

I felt the floor sag underneath my feet. I pressed my foot down hard and the floor gave way slightly. I bent down and brushed back the straw. There was wood beneath, but it was soft and wet and I was able to dig into it with my finger.

"Nicholas where are you?" I yelled.

"Down here!" he answered.

"Where?"

"Over here."

I caught sight of movement. It was Nicholas' head poking out from what appeared to be a passage to a lower level.

"Over here, there are stairs leading below. The rain isn't coming in down here."

I moved until I stood right above him and fixed him with my best angry glare, the one mom uses. I swear it can peel paint off a wall.

"Nicholas Fraser, you get right back up here this instant!"

He looked at me and cocked his head slightly to one side. "No."

"What do you mean, 'no'?"

"No...as in the opposite of yes."

"Nicholas...."

"Come on Sarah, there's nothing wrong with exploring a little. Besides, it's dry down here and safe. Don't you remember? When there's a tornado it's best to go into a basement?"

"Tornado? What tornado?" I questioned. "You said there wasn't any tornado."

"Me? What do I know about tornados? I'm just a ten year old kid, remember? All I know is I've never seen lightning or heard rain like this before in my life."

I looked around. It was now as black as night outside and the sound of the rain against the roof was deafening.

"Come, on, Sarah. It's only partially underground. There are windows that let in some light, but be careful on the steps," Nicholas said as he started down again.

The stairs were steep, crooked and old. They were covered with loose straw. I held onto the thin old railing and carefully descended the steps. With each step I moved down, a shiver ran up my spine. I reached the bottom and looked around. It was much darker than up above. While there were a few windows, they were caked over with dirt and grime, and only a little light leaked in. My eyes hadn't time to adjust to the darkness and except for the little pools of light gathered at the bottom of the stairs and in front of the windows, I couldn't see anything except shadows.

What I did notice was the difference in the air. Upstairs, wind blew through the cracks and gaps but here it seemed trapped. The air was stale and still. It was also warmer. It was good to get away from the blare of the rain. The noise still trickled down the rickety old stairs, but it was almost quiet here.

Soon my eyes were able to pick up more than just shadows. I could make out lines and edges and shades of gray. The walls were lined with empty stalls, bars imbedded in a low concrete wall. The bars were rusty and chipped but I could see flecks of their once silver paint. Between the bars were cobwebs, hundreds of them. Suspended in those webs were pieces of straw.

"Look at all the bales of hay in this basement," Nicholas said.

I looked over at him. "This isn't a basement, Nicholas. It's called a stable."

"Yeah, yeah, whatever."

He hated me correcting him—almost as much as I *loved* doing it.

Nicholas waded into a thick pile of hay that was almost waist deep. Behind him were bales, carefully piled to the ceiling. I walked over until I was standing on the outskirts of the scattered pile.

"HERE, CATCH!" Nicholas screamed as he threw a handful of straw up into the air, but missed my face. He shrieked and threw himself backwards into the pile, burrowed down into it until he disappeared from view. I could make out a wave of movement through the straw as he burrowed underneath it, towards me. I backed up. He can't sneak up on me. When he broke through, by my feet, I'd give him a little tap on the top of his head with my foot. He kept moving closer. I could see the straw parting, but still couldn't see him underneath it. The bump moved closer and closer. I drew back my foot. I was going to give him a good one. I raised my foot and the straw parted and...I opened my mouth to scream, but no sound came out. I watched in horror as a snake—a large, brown snake as thick as my arm—came out of the straw...curving and undulating...right under my raised foot...and as the head passed under me, more and more snake kept coming and coming and coming until the tail appeared and then disappeared. My whole body shuddered and I spun around, still standing on one foot as the snake disappeared into the darkness.

"Nicholas," I said, his name pushing feebly free. I lowered my foot and took a small step backwards.

"Nicholas," I called out, this time a little louder. I took another small step backwards, my eyes still fixated on the spot where the snake had vanished into the gloom. Why hadn't my brother answered? Was he all right?

"NIICCHHOLLAASS!" I screamed so loud that I felt it in my ears, and then, like peddling a bike, I raced backwards across the barn until I thumped against a cattle stall, my feet going out from under me so that I slid down the bars until I sat on the straw-littered floor.

Nicholas popped his head up out of the straw. "What's wrong now, Sarah," he asked with disdain. "Are you going to tell me I have to clean up the place 'cause I made such a mess?"

I raised my hand to point to where the snake had gone. "A snake," I muttered.

"A snake? You yelled like that because of a snake?"

"Big snake," I stammered in broken English.

"Big? Where did it go? Maybe I can catch it," he asked as he stood up and started to wade out of the pile. "How big was it?"

As I opened my mouth to answer I felt something on the back of my neck. A burst of hot air...and then another...and then another. I wanted to turn around, to look, but my head wouldn't listen and my eyes remained fixed. Another burst of air...like a breath, and then a sound, like puffing. Something, soft and gentle, but definitely something, touched my shoulder.

"Where did it go, Sarah?"

Nicholas' words broke my trance. Slowly, ever so slowly, I started to move. My back remained against the bars and I turned my head. There, just a few inches away, on the other side of the bars, were two large, golden glowing eyes.

"Come on Sarah, don't be such a baby!" Nicholas screamed at me. "Where did the snake go?"

Just then a flash of lightning filled the sky and the light forced its way in through the grimy windows, filling the stable with a micro-second of eerie brightness.

My heart stopped. I was staring, eyeball to eyeball, with a tiger, separated by a few inches of air and a couple of rusty old bars. I looked down. On my shoulder rested an enormous brown paw.

"AAAAAAAAAAAAAAAHHHHHHHHHHHHHH!" I jumped forward onto my hands and knees and scrambled on all fours, still screaming as I motored across the floor. *Thud*. I bashed into something and came to a stop. Head down, I stayed on my hands and knees, straining to catch my breath, my chest heaving up and down, up and down. In the darkness my eyes started to focus. They widened in surprise and then terror as I realized what I was seeing: two feet. I allowed my eyes to follow up from the feet and legs, leaning back to find myself looking up at a man, an old man, standing above me, holding a rifle.

"You're in more trouble than you can even imagine," he growled as he stared down at me.

Chapter 2

"Didn't you think that I'd catch you sooner or later if you kept coming back?" the old man questioned, glaring down at me with hard, angry eyes.

I looked up wordlessly. His face was lined with wrinkles and a few days worth of grey whiskers. His hair was also grey and longish and messy.

"Get up!" he ordered and prodded me with the barrel of the gun. I rose to my feet. I was shocked to realize I was taller than he was.

"What were you doing to my animals?"

"We weren't doing anything. We were just trying to get out of the rain."

"We? How many others are there?"

"Just...just my...my brother."

"COME HERE, BROTHER!" he yelled out, "or you may become an only child."

No answer came out of the gloom. The man took a few steps backwards, his eyes still trained on me. He reached over his head and I heard a 'click'. There was a soft humming sound, followed immediately by the glow of fluorescent lights. Within seconds the entire floor was bathed in light. The first thing that caught my eye was my brother, backed off in a corner, looking suitably scared.

"Come on boy!" he ordered and my brother started to slowly wade through the pile of straw. "And hurry up or I'll let my tiger come on over to get you."

Nicholas cast an anxious eye towards the tiger and then picked up his pace, hurrying over to stand beside me.

"I got to figure out what to do with you two. Maybe I should just call your parents, or the police, or maybe I should do something else." There was an ominous tone in his voice.

"Like what?" Nicholas asked. There was a catch in his voice like he was close to tears.

"I don't rightly know, but I guess there's just no telling what 'crazy old McCurdy' might do, hey?"

I swallowed hard. I looked over at Nicholas. He looked like he was about to start crying.

"Isn't that what all the kids in town call me, 'crazy old McCurdy'?"

"I don't know," I answered quite truthfully. I didn't even know any of the kids in town yet. "We just moved here two weeks ago."

"Why do you kids come up here, anyway? You trying to hurt my animals?"

"No sir," I answered, "we were trying to get out of the rain. Honestly."

"We all would have been better off if you stayed in town."

"We didn't come from town," Nicholas answered.

"Where'd you come from then?" the old man asked.

"We live on a farm just over there," I answered, pointing in the general direction of home.

"A farm? You live around here?"

"Yes, we just moved here, with our mother."

"Where is this farm?" he asked, even more forcefully.

"It's just over from here, north, the first farm," Nicholas answered.

"The Gibbons' place?"

"Yes," I answered.

He shook his head sadly. "That didn't take long. Poor woman's hardly in the ground before somebody takes over her land."

"We didn't take it over," I protested. "We inherited it."

"Inherited?"

"Yes, Mrs. Gibbons is, I mean was, our grandmother, our mother's mother."

"You're the grandchildren of Emily Gibbons?"

"Yes," both Nicholas and I answered in unison.

"My name is Sarah Fraser and this is my brother Nicholas."

He stared past us at the tiger. "I want to make sure my 'boy' is okay." He brushed between me and Nicholas and walked to the tiger's pen. He was slightly bent over and he limped as he moved. He leaned his gun against the pen and crouched down. He reached his hand between the bars. The tiger moved closer and pushed up against him. I watched in wide eyed amazement.

"PURMFFFF," the tiger said loudly.

"What was that?" Nicholas asked apprehensively.

He turned around to face us. "That's called 'puffing' and it's a greeting. Old Buddha was just saying hello."

"Ah, hello," I answered back.

"I know what to do with you two now. Come on, both of ya, up to the house." He stood up, picked up his gun and came toward us.

"I don't think we can do that," I answered. "We're not supposed to go into the house of a stranger."

"Ya better come along," he said as he brushed past us, this time in the other direction.

"But..." I started to say in objection.

"Sarah, are you crazy? He has a gun, remember?" Nicholas whispered to me.

"Yeah, I do have a gun. Here," he said, turning around and offering the weapon to Nicholas. "Carry this."

"No!" I said, stepping in between and pushing the gun back into his hands. "Mom wouldn't want him to be holding a gun."

"Why not?" the old man asked.

"Because he could get hurt, or hurt somebody else."

"The only way that could happen is if he dropped it and it landed on his foot. It ain't even loaded. And even if it was loaded, all it could do would be to put somebody to sleep."

"Sleep?" Nicholas asked.

"Yep. It's a tranquilizer gun."

"What would you want with a gun like that?" Nicholas questioned.

"They're for putting large animals to sleep so they can be trapped, or treated or examined," I answered.

"Does she always answer everybody's questions?" the old man asked Nicholas.

"Yeah, but you get used to it after a while."

"And is she usually right?"

"Almost always," my brother confirmed. "What would happen if you shot a man with one of these?"

The old man turned to me. "You wanta answer that one or should I?"

"I don't know the answer."

"Good!" the old man chortled, and Nicholas chuckled as well. "If you shot a man he'd go down just like any other animal. Depending on how big he was, and how big a dose was in the gun, he'd just go to sleep. Course he'd wake up with a headache that'd make him think his head was going to split right in two," he chuckled. "Believe me!"

"You've shot somebody with one before?" Nicholas asked.

"Yeah...me."

"You shot yourself!" Nicholas exclaimed.

"Yep, and the worst part was that I had nobody else to blame. I was carrying the rifle, tripped and it went off. The needle went right through the shoe and into my foot. Slept for the better part of two days," he chuckled even louder. "Enough story telling, come on up to the house and let me have a look at that knee."

"Knee, what knee?" I asked.

He pointed at my leg. I looked down. My left pant leg was ripped and blood was dripping out of the tear.

"Come on, we'll fix you up," he said and then turned and started walking away.

I trailed after him reluctantly.

We left the barn and took the gravel path. It had stopped raining and a few strands of sunlight had burst through the clouds. There was a small trickle of water rolling down the hill beside the barn.

"Close the door after you," he yelled over his shoulder without looking back.

I turned around to Nicholas who was just leaving the barn and ordered him to do the same. I quickly hobbled alongside of him, trying to keep up. He glanced over at me but didn't change his expression.

"Did you know our grandmother?" I asked.

"First met her when I was about seven years old," he answered softly.

"We didn't know her very well. She didn't like travelling that much, especially the last couple of years when she wasn't feeling very well. We only saw her on special holidays and things like that."

He nodded his head, but didn't say anything.

"Do you know my mother?"

"Nope. Knew that Emmy had children, but I never met any of them."

"I thought you'd know my mother for sure. She was raised in the farmhouse where we're living."

"My brother would have known her, but I wasn't around. I just got back myself about six months ago."

"Our Nana died about four months ago," Nicholas said from behind.

"Yep," he answered.

"Is it just you and your brother living here?" I asked.

"Nope. Just me. My brother died about a year ago."

"I'm sorry," I said.

"That's okay. None of it seems too real anyhow. It had been almost forty years since I'd seen him."

"Wow!" Nicholas exclaimed. "How come?" he questioned.

"Nicholas! It's not polite to ask!"

"That's okay. The only thing my brother and I had in common was our parents. Both of my parents died over forty years ago. My brother stayed and ran the farm and there wasn't really any reason for me to come back home."

As we got closer to the house I realized it wasn't in much better shape than the barn. Mr. McCurdy grabbed the old screen door and pulled it open.

"Coming in?" he asked.

"I...I guess so," I answered.

He let go of the door and it jumped back noisily into the frame.

"Come on," I said to Nicholas.

"I didn't think you wanted us to go into a stranger's house."

"He knew Nana. Besides, who's scared now?" I asked. I opened the door and went into the house with Nicholas following closely on my heels. I was immediately hit by a wave of foul air.

"What died in here?" Nicholas asked.

"SSSSHHHH," I scolded.

We walked down a dimly lit hall tracking a trail of mud along the length of the hall to the kitchen. There was a table, littered with newspapers, dirty dishes and assorted other things surrounded by four old chairs. A large black wooden stove sat in the far corner. My eyes were still wandering the room when Mr. McCurdy came back into the kitchen through a doorway at the far side.

"Sit down," he ordered.

I moved over to one of the chairs and pulled it out from

the table. It was covered with a thick pile of old, yellowed newspapers. I pulled out a second chair and sat down. He walked over, carrying a little white box, and bent down beside me.

"Let's see if we can fix that cut."

"I guess you hadn't seen Nana for a long time if you were away so long," I hinted.

"A long time. Meant to drop in and see her, but I just kept putting it off and putting it off and then...I read about it in the papers...the funeral."

"OOOCCHH!" I screamed, clutching my leg.

"Sorry. I didn't know it would sting so badly." He paused. "I almost went to the funeral, but then I thought...I wouldn't. I didn't want to change the way I remembered her," he said wistfully.

"I don't understand," I said.

"You're too young to understand. You see, when you haven't seen somebody for a long time you keep a picture of them in your mind. You may grow old, but that picture doesn't age."

"And you have a picture of our Nana in your mind?" I asked.

"I sure do. I remember a picnic, just at the end of the school year. It was a beautiful day, sunny, not a cloud in the sky. Warm, maybe even hot. Everybody was spreading out their blankets and setting out their lunches. There was a baseball game going on, off in one corner. Almost everybody was there, but not your Nana. Then suddenly she came waltzing into the field. Heads turned. She knew how to move so just enough of her ankles showed under that dress," he chuckled and shook his head.

"Ankles?" Nicholas questioned.

"They wore long dresses back then," I answered.

"That's right. She wore a long blue dress with red flowers on it. She wore a big straw hat too, tied with a ribbon, a pink ribbon, and...."

"You remember what she was wearing?" I asked.

"You have to remember she wasn't just any girl. She was the most beautiful girl in the whole school."

"Nana?"

"For you she'll always be Nana. For me she'll be a beautiful young girl strolling through the meadow, smiling and laughing."

"The laughing and smiling part sounds like her," I said.

"It's wonderful that didn't change. When I close my eyes I can still picture her in that meadow, still so young."

Mr. McCurdy's eyes were closed. His face looked peaceful. Then he opened his eyes again and I looked away, embarrassed that our gazes had met.

"How long ago was that? How old was she?" Nicholas asked.

"That was so long ago it'll seem like forever to you two, but to me it was just the blink of an eye. Sixty years ago. She was fourteen, or maybe even fifteen. No, she had to be fourteen, because we were born the same year, and I ran away to join the circus the summer I was fourteen."

"You ran away to join the circus!" my brother said excitedly.

Mr. McCurdy took a large pad of gauze and taped it in place over my knee. "Maybe 'ran away' wasn't quite right. At that age you could pretty well do what you wanted and I wanted to be with the circus, wanted to lead an exciting life: travelling, seeing the world, big crowds, new people, always on the move."

"It sounds exciting!" Nicholas blurted out. "Were you like an acrobat, or a juggler, or did you get shot out of a canon, or—"

"Animals."

"Animals?"

"Yep, animals. I took care of the animals."

"That must have been pretty exciting too," I said encouragingly.

"If you consider shovelling elephant crap or cleaning out tiger cages exciting, then it sure enough was. But, I did a lot more than that after the first few years."

"Like what?" I asked.

"I also trained them and kept them warm and safe, used to treat them when they were sick. Hardly a vet around who knows what to do when an elephant has problems, but I do. I was there to help when they gave birth and to take over raising them if anything happened to the mother. Many a time I've had to have a little tiger, born too early, snuggled up with me for nights on end feeding it out of an eye dropper."

"Wow!" I gasped. I loved animals, but we'd never been able to have anything except fish because of all my father's allergies.

"Mama, God rest her soul, told me that if I joined the circus that I'd never settle down, that I'd never be able to get married or raise a family. She was right. Mothers are almost always right. But you know, when you spend as much time as I did with those animals, they get to be like your family and when you raise them from little balls of wet fur, they feel like they're yours."

"What sort of animals?" I asked.

"You already met one kind, up close," he scoffed, laughing

a bit before the laugh turned into a coughing fit.

"Too close," I said. "But worse than the tiger was that snake."

"You met my snake did you! You don't have to worry about him. That snake isn't big enough to harm anybody."

"Not big enough?" I said increduously. "It looked pretty big to me."

"It is pretty big. It's almost nine feet long, but that's not big enough to harm anyone except a wee child."

"I still wouldn't want it to bite me," Nicholas said.

"You don't have to worry about that. It wouldn't bite you. It would wrap itself around you. Then it squeezes and squeezes, tighter and tighter until you can't breathe. Then it eats you, whole, swallows you down in one gulp."

"Gross," my brother said.

"When it swallows you you're not even dead yet. In South America there was a lady swallowed by a snake. They found the snake quickly and cut her out of it's belly and she lived. Or so they say."

"Wow. Talk about lucky!" I exclaimed.

"I don't know. I don't think it's ever so lucky to get swallowed alive," he responded.

"But at least she lived. At least it all ended happily," I emphasized.

"Maybe for the lady...but not for the snake. I just can't help but thinking about Brent, cut open from one end to the other."

"Brent?" I asked.

"That's my snake."

"What kind of snake is 'Brent'?" Nicholas asked.

"He's a Burmese Python."

"What does he eat?" I asked.

"Snake Chow," my brother answered.

Mr. McCurdy chuckled. "I don't recall seeing that on the shelf at the grocery store. What he eats mostly is rats and mice. He keeps them under control in the barn."

"Most people keep a couple of cats to do that," Nicholas said.

"Yep. Sometimes there'll be the odd cat 'round the barn. City folks just drop them off, thinking they can live alone in the country."

"I guess the cats catch mice too," I suggested.

"Imagine so. They don't stay around very long though," he answered.

"How come?" I asked, and then the answer came to me.

"Snake chow, you might say, although I really can't say for sure," Mr. McCurdy replied. "I don't see much of Brent these days. He spends all his time in the barn, chasing down mice or bedding down under the straw. He used to stay mostly here in the house, would snuggle down at the foot of my bed, underneath the covers."

I made a face like I was going to gag. Mr. McCurdy looked at me and shook his head.

"Let me guess. You probably think that snakes are all slimy?"

"Well...not really. I just...."

"Probably never held one. Have you, Nicholas?"

"Sometimes, but not ever one that big," Nicholas answered hesitantly.

"Well, remind me to introduce you to Brent, maybe even pick him up. He's as soft and warm as a pair of old leather shoes. Gentle as a kitten too."

"How about if I just pick up a kitten?" I asked.

"She isn't a kitten any more but if you want gentle you can't beat that old girl in the corner there," he said, pointing.

Both Nicholas and I followed his finger. Lying on the couch was a large animal.

"It's another tiger!" Nicholas yelled, backing away.

"No, it's a cheetah," I corrected him, but backed away as well.

"How do you know about cheetahs?" Mr. McCurdy asked.

"I read about them. You know, from National Geographic and books. They're really fast—"

"The fastest animal on this planet. They take off and before you can count to five they're travelling faster than any car along the highway."

"That's amazing," Nicholas said.

"And do you know why they can run that fast?" Mr. McCurdy asked.

"The secret's in the spine. It's whole back from the top of the head to the tip of the tail is like one big spring," I answered.

Mr. McCurdy and Nicholas exchanged looks. "You get used to her knowing everything after a while," Nicholas said.

"Laura, wake up!" Mr. McCurdy barked.

The cat turned its head to one side and its eye opened up.

"Laura, come on over here," he ordered.

The cat closed its eye and turned its head away.

"Laura you come here this minute!" he hollered, louder.

Once again the cat turned to face us and its eyes opened. Lazily it rolled off the chesterfield and landed on the floor. It stretched, its back dipping downward, almost touching its belly to the ground. It shuffled across the floor and then plopped down, right in front of Mr. McCurdy, on his feet, and continued its nap.

"Boy that was fast," Nicholas said sarcastically.

"She's an old girl. If she was a human she'd be even older than me and I don't run races any more. Still, once she stretches out the old muscles she could run faster than any other animal, young or old, except for maybe a gazelle or a deer. Come here, I want you to feel something."

We both hesitated, exchanging looks.

"Don't be afraid. This is a cheetah, not a tiger. Cheetahs aren't like other big cats. Tigers, lions, cougars, leopards and jaguars, you can't really trust one hundred percent. Even if you raised them from a kit, even if you're their friend, even if you never ever saw them do one thing wrong, you still can't trust them completely. You turn your back and WHACK," he smacked his hand on the table and both Nicholas and I jumped in our seats.

"They smack you on the neck. Maybe they only mean it as a little love tap, but you're dead just the same. But Laura is different," he said, motioning to the cat, asleep on the floor, covering his feet, who hadn't even raised an eyebrow in response to the noise.

"Cheetahs are more like dogs. They like people, want to make them happy. See these claws," he said, lifting up one of her front feet. "Other cats, even little house cats, have sheaths where they keep their claws when they're not using them. Cheetahs don't have those. Their claws are always out, like studs in snow tires, to give better traction. Everything about them is designed for speed.

"They aren't big like the other big cats. Can't be big *and* fast, and speed is everything with them. You need to be fast, not sneaky or strong, to outrun your lunch. A cheetah, sometimes a pair of them, gets close to a herd, usually gazelles, and then just bursts after them, running at top speed. For a little while, maybe one or two hundred yards, it's the fastest. If it doesn't make a catch by then it just stops and waits for another chance. It can't run that fast for long.

"The way they catch their food, chasing it down like that, is more like canines—you know, wolves or dogs or jackals—than it is like the other cats. The ancient Egyptians used them as hunting dogs. I read somewhere about a Pharaoh who had fifty pairs of hunting cheetahs."

"What's that sound?" Nicholas asked.

"Sound? Oh, that's Laura. She's purring."

"Purring?"

"Yep. Let's you know that she's happy. Probably having a good dream."

"Maybe thinking about running free in Africa," I suggested.

"That would be some dream. She was born here, in the back of a circus truck."

"Really? You're kidding," Nicholas said.

"Of course, 'really'. I got too many stories I've lived to need to make up anything. Half of what I've seen I can't ever tell anybody because they wouldn't believe me."

"I didn't mean I thought you were lying," Nicholas apologized.

"That's okay, it's just I'm a little touchy about this. You see, cheetahs are shy, and they don't like to breed except in the wild. Big zoos run by people with all kinds of fancy degrees spend all sorts of money to try to get that to happen. It used to drive them crazy that some guy who didn't finish grade ten could do it, in a travelling circus. Over the years Laura and I, and her mother and her aunt before her, gave birth to, and raised, twenty-seven cheetahs."

"Twenty-seven! What happened to them? What happened to the babies?"

"Sold them to zoos around the world."

"Too bad they couldn't be let go into the wild," Nicholas said and then, judging from the look in his eyes, realized he'd probably said something wrong again.

"You're probably right. There's more cheetahs in zoos now than in the wild, but you can't take a cheetah raised in captivity and turn it lose. It just wouldn't know what to do."

"You stupid idiot!" came a voice from the other room.

I jumped slightly out of my seat and all three of us swivelled our heads to face the doorway leading out of the kitchen.

"Be quiet you old feather brain!" hollered Mr. McCurdy.

"Stupid old man!" came the reply through the doorway.

Mr. McCurdy shook his head. "If you want to insult me, at least come and face me!"

"Ugly old man!"

"Don't get me mad," Mr. McCurdy threatened.

"Drop dead!"

"That's it," said Mr. McCurdy. He rose from his seat, walked across the kitchen, and opened a cupboard. He reached up and pulled out a box.

"Want some crackers?" he called out, and opened up the box.

A flash of blue and yellow came hurtling through the

doorway as a large parrot flew into the room, flapped around, skimming over our heads and finally landed on his shoulder.

"Give me grub!" the parrot ordered.

"No way!" Mr. McCurdy replied. "Be polite and say hello to our guests."

The parrot turned its head so that one large eye was facing directly towards us sitting at the table. Making contact, it spun its head around and stared at us with the other eye.

"Greet our guests," Mr. McCurdy ordered.

"Hello...ugly children!" it squawked.

Mr. McCurdy burst into laughter as both Nicholas and I gasped in shock.

"Stupid bird," Nicholas said.

"Stupid boy," replied the bird.

"No point in trying to get into an argument with him. The bird always gets in the last word, unless of course I do this." Mr. McCurdy handed the bird a large cracker which it took with a foot and quickly placed into its mouth.

"That'll keep him quiet for a minute."

"Why did you train your parrot to insult people?" Nicholas asked.

"Firstly, it's not a parrot but a Military Maquaw, and secondly, it was saying these words long before I came along."

"But..." I started to say and then stopped myself.

"But how could anything, other than a dinosaur, have been on this earth before me?"

"I didn't..." I stammered.

"Sure, sure, sure. People don't know some birds live to be real old. Parrots and maquaws can live to be one hundred and twenty-five years old. This fellow has to be at least a hundred years old."

"Wow, he doesn't look that old," I blurted out.

"And just how would you expect an old bird to look? Gray feathers? Wrinkled forehead? Balding? Hobbling around?"

"Shut up, stupid!" the bird called out.

"All right, I'll shut up. Here have another cracker," he offered the bird.

"Maybe you should only feed it when it says nice things," suggested Nicholas.

"If I only fed him when he was polite there'd only be a bag of feather-covered bones on my shoulder here. Maquaws aren't just smart, but stubborn as well."

"If he's so smart, couldn't you teach him some good things to say?" Nicholas questioned.

"I have. I trained him to say lots of things. He probably has more than ninety words he can say...when he wants to. Usually all he says is insults. The older he gets the more cranky he gets. Then again, so do I."

As we watched, the bird walked down Mr. McCurdy's arm and stuck its head inside the box of crackers. Its head reappeared with a cracker sticking out of the corner of its beak.

"What's your parrot, I mean your maquaw's, name?" Nicholas asked.

"Polly," he answered, with disgust in his voice.

"Polly?"

"Yep. It wasn't my idea. Some foolish sailor, who's probably been dead for fifty years, hung that name on him."

"Why don't you change it?" I questioned.

"It's not for me to do. That's the bird's name and I can't change that any more than I could change your name if I didn't like it."

"Dirty, smelly ape," Polly said.

"Hey!" answered Nicholas.

"I can see how you'd think that he was smart," I taunted, "that's what I think of Nicholas too."

"He wasn't talking to your brother," Mr. McCurdy said.

Nicholas started to laugh. "Must be you," my brother said, pointing at me.

"Wrong again," Mr. McCurdy said. "I think he's referring to that dirty smelly ape standing behind you in the doorway."

We spun around to see a monkey squatting in the doorway, looking squarely at us, a big toothy smile on his face. As we watched in wide-eyed shock, it rose to its feet, knuckles still dragging on the ground, and walked into the kitchen. It moved across the floor and opened the door to the fridge, the open door mostly hiding it from view.

"PFFFFT," came a sound from behind the door. The chimp took a step back and I could see that he was holding a can of Coke. He tipped it to his mouth and drank thirstily.

"Calvin! What are you doing?" Mr. McCurdy yelled.

The chimp, I guess his name was Calvin, lowered the can. He stared at Mr. McCurdy with a look that I could only describe as thoughtful.

"Where are your manners? Shouldn't you offer our company a drink?" he asked.

Calvin extended his arm, the one holding the Coke, in our direction.

"No Calvin, they don't want to share your drink. They want their own."

Calvin drew his arm back in. He put his can on the floor

and took two steps backwards to the fridge, the door again shielding him from our view. "PFFFFFT!...PPPPFFFFFT!"

Calvin reappeared, a can of Coke in each of his hands. His face was distorted into a huge grin. Large yellowing teeth showed between his oversized lips.

"Close the door," Mr. McCurdy ordered.

Calvin had both hands full and he reached back with one foot, while balancing on the other, and pushed the door closed. With a can in each hand, he wasn't able to use them to move and he walked awkwardly, swinging one leg and then the other. He lumbered across the kitchen floor until he stood right in front of us. He looked me squarely in the eyes. The teeth disappeared as his smile was replaced by a serious look. He tilted his head to one side and then the other.

"What's he doing?" I asked nervously.

"I don't know," Mr. McCurdy answered. "Maybe just checking you out a bit."

"Probably thinks he sees a family resemblance," Nicholas laughed.

I jumped in my seat as Calvin threw back his head and joined Nicholas in a loud laugh.

"He thinks I'm funny!" Nick said proudly.

Calvin thrust his arms out and offered me a Coke. Carefully I reached forward to take it. I felt a little unnerved when my hand and his met around the can. I tried to pull the can free but he didn't loosen his grip.

"Ahh...Mr. McCurdy...?"

"Show your manners," he answered softly.

"Manners?"

"Weren't you taught to say please and thank you?"

"Yeah...um...thanks Calvin," I muttered. Instantly he released his grip. He shuffled over and offered the second can to Nicholas

"Thanks, Calvin," Nicholas said and the Coke was released.

"How about one for me?" Mr. McCurdy asked.

Calvin turned and looked at Mr. McCurdy. He put his hands up to his ears, spread them like antlers, stuck out his tongue and went "PPPPLLLLLLEEEEEEEZZZZ," and a fine mist of saliva shot out of his mouth. Mr. McCurdy broke into a full laugh that was only broken by another coughing fit. Calvin, his hands now free, quickly moved across the floor, grabbed his Coke, squatted down and took another long sip. A little dribble flowed down out of the corner of his mouth and disappeared into his fur.

"Should he be drinking pop?" I asked.

"Why not? Chimps aren't much different than people. Besides, it's like that joke: Where does a nine hundred pound gorilla sleep? Anywhere it wants. So, I guess he can drink what he wants."

"But he's just a chimp. He couldn't hurt anybody," I said.

"HUH!" Mr. McCurdy stated. He turned directly to Nicholas. "It must feel good to know she doesn't know everything."

My brother nodded his head in agreement.

"A full grown chimp, like Calvin here, is strong enough to rip a man apart. He could practically tear your arm right off. Even lions leave a healthy male chimpanzee alone."

I looked over at Calvin, reclining on his back on the floor, a now empty Coke can balanced on one of his back feet, sticking up in the air.

"Him?" Nicholas asked.

"Him," Mr. McCurdy answered. "Calvin...act mean."

Calvin closed his eyes and scratched under his left arm pit with his right hand.

"Pretty mean," Nicholas chuckled.

Mr. McCurdy shook his head. "CALVIN..."

Calvin opened his eyes.

"Calvin, you mangy monkey, if you don't act mean, right now, I'll...."

I watched as Calvin's eyes opened. He quickly rolled over and got to his feet. His teeth, which I'd seen when he smiled, once again became visible but now he snarled menacingly.

"EEEEEEEEEHHHHHHHHHHH," he screamed and started to beat an arm against his chest. With his free hand he grabbed the empty coke can and tossed it across the room. It bounced on the table top, careened off the wall and dropped to the floor.

I felt my heart rise into my throat and then stop beating completely.

Calvin moved threateningly toward us, opened his mouth wide, showing all his teeth and then, "BUURRRPP!" Calvin looked embarrassed and sat down by our feet.

"Sometimes the Coke gives him a little gas," Mr. McCurdy explained.

As if in answer, Nicholas burped as well.

Everybody broke into laughter. I looked at my watch. It was time to go home and I didn't want to be late.

"We better get going." I rose to my feet. "It was really nice to meet you, and your animals."

"It was really nice meeting the two of you. What do you

know, the grandchildren of Emmy Gibbons. You know, you even look like her," he said to me.

"She does?" Nicholas asked. "I thought you said that our Nana was really beautiful."

"Shut up, stupid boy!" Polly squawked.

I smiled. "Thank you, Polly."

"You're welcome...stupid girl," Polly replied.

We left the kitchen and walked down the hallway. Mr. McCurdy followed after us. I stopped at the door.

"Don't go trying any more short-cuts, you hear?"

"Yes sir," I answered.

"Just go straight down my driveway and along the road," he ordered.

"Sure, no problem," Nicholas agreed.

We exchanged good-byes and left. The gravel path crunched under my feet. The sky was now clear and the sun was shining again. I heard the screen door slam and looked back. Mr. McCurdy was standing there, watching us walk away. I stopped. Nicholas kept on walking.

"And thanks for the drink and for fixing up my knee," I called back.

"That's just being a good neighbour," he said with a wave of his hand.

"Is it okay for one neighbour to drop in and see another neighbour sometime?" I asked. I held my breath waiting for an answer.

"Nope, its not okay...it's much better than okay," he said and smiled. "Any time."

"Great. Well good-bye. I mean, I'll see you later," I said and then sprinted to catch up to Nicholas.

Chapter 3

We moved quickly along the road. I wanted to get home and cleaned up before Mom arrived.

"Pretty weird, eh?" Nicholas asked.

"Different."

"You going to go back?"

"Yeah. Why not?"

"I don't know. The animals are pretty cool, but he's strange," Nicholas observed.

"Like I said, he's different."

"If Mom knew she wouldn't let you go back there."

"Why not? Why wouldn't she want me to visit an elderly man who's our neighbor and knew our grandmother?" I asked innocently.

Nicholas smiled at me. "So what you're saying is that you think we should lie."

"No, I'm not saying we should lie!"

"So you think we should tell her about the gun and the tiger and python and...."

"No!" I interrupted. "I'm just saying that we shouldn't tell her everything. There's no point in worrying her, is there?"

"It's good to see that I've finally had an influence on you," Nicholas chuckled, "a bad influence."

"Don't be ridiculous," I countered. We turned off the road and onto the long driveway up to our house which was still hidden around a curve in the lane.

"Be careful, Sarah. Telling lies is just like eating pretzels. It's hard to stop after just one."

"I'm not telling any lies!"

"The best lie is half the truth."

"Oh shoot!" I exclaimed. "Look who's here."

Parked next to the house was a bright, lime green car that belonged to our sitter, Erin. If she was here that meant Mom was working late. Again.

Nicholas opened the door. I took a deep breath and followed after him. We were greeted by the sound of Erin's voice. She was talking on the phone.

I went to the cupboard to see what I could make for supper. Erin continued to talk on the phone, as if we weren't even there. As I shuffled cans and containers I picked up enough of the conversation to figure out she was talking to a boyfriend. Probably a new boyfriend. She always had a new boyfriend. My mother would be happy if Nicholas changed his socks as often as Erin changed boyfriends. She finally glanced our way.

"I guess I should be going now," she said into the phone, and then turned her back to us and made a kissing sound.

"Oh yuck," my brother said with his mouth full of peanut butter he'd spooned out of the jar.

Erin hung up and turned to us.

"Your mother called. She said she wouldn't be home until late tonight. I'm to feed you and get you both into bed."

I opened my mouth to say something, but closed it again. I'd been trying to be nicer to Erin but it was hard. It just bugged me to have her tell me what to do. I knew that she was older, she was almost seventeen, but she was just so...so....

"Erin, do you know our neighbor, Mr. McCurdy?" Nicholas asked.

"Old man McCurdy?"

"I imagine he has a first name," I answered curtly.

"Yeah, that's him," Nicholas said ignoring me. "He's a real old guy. Do you know him?"

"Not really, but I know of him," Erin answered, "or should I say I know about his family."

"Fill us in," my brother invited.

"Well...everybody in town knows about the McCurdy family. They were always a little strange. There used to be stories about what went on at the farm. You know, ghost stories."

"Ghost stories?" I questioned.

"They said the place was haunted, that old McCurdy was into strange voodoo things." She looked like she was actually a little spooked just talking about it.

"Come on, Erin, you don't actually believe all those stories?"

"Maybe not all of them, but I've got friends who've seen things...."

"Yeah, everybody always has a 'friend' who has a 'friend' who knows somebody who saw something," I scoffed. "But did you ever see anything?"

"Well...I didn't actually see anything."

I flashed a smug smile at Nicholas.

"But I was up there when...."

"You've been to the farm?" I interrupted.

"Well..." she answered, her voice just above a whisper. "Once."

"When was that?" Nicholas asked.

"Promise you won't tell anybody?" she asked, again in a low voice.

"Who do you think we're going to tell?" Nicholas said.

"I don't know, but promise me what I say will just be between the three of us."

"Sure no problem," Nicholas answered.

She looked at me. I nodded in agreement.

"It was a couple of years ago. One of my boyfriends used to go up there sometimes...late at night...and wander around the farm and the fields. It was a dare, and I went up with him."

"And?" I asked.

"And what?"

"And what did you see?"

"See? I didn't really see anything, but I could tell that evil things were going on."

"How could you tell?" I asked.

"I just knew. I'm one of those people who are very sensitive to things like that. Spirits and ghosts and U.F.O.s. I think I even have E.S.P."

"I knew you were going to say that," Nicholas deadpanned.

I gave him a dirty look.

"And I knew that you'd give me that look," he continued.

"What?" Erin asked.

"Nothing," he chuckled. "So you think you have extra sensory perception?"

I bit my tongue to stop from laughing.

"Either way, if that was a few years ago, then you would have been up there when the other brother was running the farm." I said.

"Yeah. But then his brother, none of us even knew he had a brother, showed up and I hear that he's even more strange."

"Strange, how?" Nicholas asked blankly.

"Bizarre sounds from the barn," she answered, her voice once again a whisper.

"I don't know how you can make claims based on rumours," I protested. "Today Nicholas and I went...."

"For a walk by old man McCurdy's farm," my brother interrupted, "and now that we know about it we won't go by there again." He gave me a knowing look. "And Erin, our mother gets spooked easily so we'd appreciate it if you didn't mention any of this to her. Okay?"

"I don't even like talking about it. It makes me nervous."

I started to get dinner ready while Erin and Nicholas went into the livingroom to watch TV. We didn't mention to Mom that I was the one fixing suppers when Erin was taking care of us. The first night she'd tried to fix us dinner, but it was inedible. After that I was the one who made supper.

"Good morning, sleepy head. Time to get up."

I turned over, recognizing Mom's voice. The bright morning light hurt my eyes as I struggled to open them.

"I see Erin took good care of you. The kitchen was even cleaned up."

Of course it was cleaned up. I did it while she was having another lengthy telephone conversation with her boyfriend.

"Erin took good care of us," I said.

"I was talking to Nicholas, he's been up for a while. He mentioned you met one of our neighbors."

I swallowed hard. "Yes."

"He said that he was a nice older man and he knew Nana."

Again I swallowed and nodded in agreement. I wonder what else Nicholas had mentioned.

"Your brother said you two thought you'd head back over to see him again some time."

"If that would be okay with you, Mom." Obviously Nicholas hadn't told her anything else, or at least anything else that would worry her.

"Why wouldn't it be okay? I think it's sweet the two of you want to spend time with a lonely old man, but there is one condition," she said slyly.

I held my breath.

"You have to tell me any stories he has about your grandmother. I heard she was quite an interesting lady when she was younger."

"Sure, no problem," I answered, exhaling.

"Better get up and get moving," Mom said as she left my room. I listened to the floor creak as she walked. She stopped in the bathroom.

The entire farm house had hardwood floors that creaked and groaned under foot. The worst part was at night. Long after we went to bed and the lights were off, the floor continued to make noises. Mom said it was like that when she was little and she used to be scared by the sounds. When Nicholas heard me say it made me nervous he started telling me stories. Now, every night I prop a chair under the doorknob just in case the floors creak because someone is coming.

I threw back the covers and hung my legs over the edge of the bed. I felt with my feet until I found my slippers, tucked in under my bed, as they always were. I slipped them on and stood up. I plumped up my pillow, put it in its place, pulled up the covers and made my bed.

I heard Mom singing. She sang a lot lately, songs from the radio, songs I liked. It scared me.

One of the first things to change with my father was the music he listened to. One day he's normal and listening to 'adult' music and then as fast as you can change the dial, he's listening to rock and roll. Next he started to wear his hair differently. My dad began to grow his hair long on one side so he could comb it over his bald spot. Then, he went out and bought a new, red, convertible sports car. And worse, he bought it without even talking it over with Mom. That was the biggest argument I'd ever heard them have. The funniest thing was watching Dad drive with the top down, his long strands of hair trailing behind him, like a horse's tail.

I strolled down the hall and peeked in the open bathroom door. Mom was standing in front of the mirror. She was wearing high-heeled shoes and a skirt that I thought was too short for either a lawyer or a mother. I watched in fascination as she started to apply her make-up. She put on this thick looking pink stuff and rubbed it into her neck and around her eyes. She told me this was to 'hide' her wrinkles. I didn't really think she had enough wrinkles to worry about hiding. She then put rouge on her cheeks and started layering on black mascara. Before my father left, she hardly wore any make-up at all. She called it the 'natural look'. I guess that meant she was now going for the 'unnatural look'.

"Do you want to try some make-up?" Mom asked.

She'd startled me. "Ah...no thanks," I mumbled.

"I'm sure a lot of girls your age, in your grade, will be wearing make-up."

"Just because a lot of girls will be wearing it doesn't mean I have to!"

My mother turned around and we exchanged strange looks. This was probably the only house in the whole country where a mother was trying to *convince* her teenage daughter to wear make-up.

"I don't think she needs to wear make-up," my brother piped up.

I turned around. I didn't even hear him come upstairs. One of his favourite new games was seeing if he could move around without causing the boards to creak so he could surprise us.

"Isn't that sweet!" Mom beamed. "Your brother thinks you're so attractive that you don't need make-up!"

"I didn't say *that*," Nicholas protested. "I meant that it wouldn't *help*." He instantly turned and ran along the hall and down the stairs.

"Do you see what I have to put up with!"

"I'll talk to him."

"Talk to him! That's all you ever do is talk to him! Why don't you punish him? Put him in his room, take away his allowance, ground him!"

"I'll talk to him," she repeated.

"I don't even tell you most of the things he does. When you get home tonight I'm going to tell you everything he did wrong today."

"You'll have to wait till tomorrow. I won't be home until you're in bed. Erin will be taking care of you two."

"Erin! Two nights of Erin in a row isn't fair," I cried. "Besides, when you come home so late I forget half of the things I want to talk to you about."

"Maybe you should write them down."

"Like in a letter?" I asked in disbelief.

"Yes, exactly, like a letter!" she exclaimed.

Great, I have a father who bounces around from place to place and the only contact I have with him is the letters he writes, but I can't write back because he keeps no fixed address. Now I have a mother, who lives in the same house with me, and she thinks I should write her letters.

"Why do we have to have Erin? Why can't I take care of us?" I asked.

"You're too young."

"But I'm not too young to take care of us all day long," I protested.

"We've been over this, Sarah. It's different during the day, but not late at night."

"Late? How late? You don't usually even work on Friday nights."

"It isn't work," she said meekly as she put in a pair of earrings. "It's a date."

"A date!"

"Yes, a date."

"Is it with that Peter guy again?" I asked.

"No. Somebody new."

"Who is he?"

"His name is Robert."

"Where did you meet him?"

"At work. He's a lawyer," she answered.

"I haven't heard you mention him before."

"He just started. I better get going," she said as she moved by me and out of the bathroom. I trailed behind her, along the hall and down the stairs.

"Isn't it unusual for a firm as small as yours to hire another lawyer so soon after you became a partner?" I asked.

"He's more like a...junior lawyer. He just graduated," she said as she pushed into the kitchen.

"Junior lawyer! How old is he?" I asked.

"Sarah, how should I know how old he is?"

"You must have some idea," I stated. "About how old is he?"

"I don't know, twenty-seven or twenty-eight, I'd imagine," she said. She looked tremendously embarrassed.

"Twenty-seven or twenty-eight! If he's twenty-seven then he's exactly half way between my age and yours," I stated.

"Sarah, age isn't important. Everybody says I look a lot younger than forty-one."

She grabbed her purse and started for the door.

"Aren't you going to have breakfast?"

"I don't have time, Sarah."

"But breakfast is the most important meal of the day," I said.

"Maybe I'll have a bigger lunch to make up for it."

She gave me a hug. "Look after your brother and I'll talk to you tomorrow," she said. She picked up her purse, grabbed her briefcase and was out the door before I could say another word. Maybe I should start writing that letter. I heard the engine start and went to the window to watch her drive out of sight.

As she disappeared out of view in one direction, Nicholas entered the kitchen from the other. He opened a cupboard door and pulled out a monster jar of peanut butter.

"Are we going over to see Mr. McCurdy before or after lunch?" he asked.

"I didn't think we were going to go at all today. Shouldn't we wait a few days so we don't appear too eager?"

"But we are eager. I don't want all that good lying I did with Mom to go to waste. Besides, if we don't go soon we might not get to go at all."

"Why not?"

"Mom may hear something about Mr. McCurdy when she's shopping or from one of the other neighbors and then she won't let us go."

"I doubt it. She doesn't seem to hear anything that anybody says to her," I said under my breath.

"What?"

"Nothing. Do you really think we should go today?" I asked.

"Definitely, but we shouldn't go empty handed."

"What should we bring?" I asked.

"Muffins. You bake some muffins and I'll take care of other business," Nicholas said.

"Other business? What other business?"

"Staying out of your way when you bake. I'll be in the livingroom watching TV."

Chapter 4

"Come on, Sarah, just one," Nicholas pleaded.

"No. How many times do I have to tell you?"

"You don't have to tell me no. Just say yes."

"No way. I can't give Mr. McCurdy eleven chocolate chip muffins. I've got to give him an even dozen."

Nicholas and I had had this same conversation each of the last three mornings as we headed over to see Mr. McCurdy. When we got to his house we'd eat the muffins and talk for a while and then go off and spend time with the animals. Most of them were okay, except for the snake which, thank God, had stayed out of sight. The tiger, Buddha, made me very nervous but he was fascinating and I loved to watch him...from outside the cage. Nicholas, of course, had to show how brave he was and had even fed Buddha some raw meat right out of his hand. I kept a safe distance. Mr. McCurdy had said a tiger could eat a hundred and ten pounds of meat at one sitting and I weighed just over a hundred pounds. I didn't like the thought that I could be a meal, and not even a complete meal.

"What difference does it make? Five minutes after we walk in he's going to offer me one," Nicholas said.

"Then no big deal. Just wait."

We walked along in silence, the only sound coming from the gravel crunching under our feet.

"Sure smells good," my brother mumbled.

"Don't you ever give up?" I said in exasperation.

"Yes."

"When?"

"When I get what I want. If you want me to stop then stuff a muffin in my mouth."

For a split second I thought it would be worth it.

"How about if you bake blueberry muffins tomorrow," Nicholas suggested. "They're Mr. McCurdy's favourite."

"They are? How do you know?"

"I just know," he answered.

"Okay, I guess I can bake blueberry for tomorrow. Wait a second. Blueberry is *your* favourite," I objected.

"What a coincidence, eh?"

"Nicholas you..." I stopped mid-sentence. We'd come to Mr. McCurdy's driveway. The wooden post that normally held his mail box, was leaning off to one side and was smashed off at the top. Looking down I saw the yellow mailbox with its faded red letters that read 'McCurdy', in the ditch.

"I wonder how that happened?" Nicholas asked. "It was here when we left yesterday, wasn't it?"

"I didn't notice."

We walked up the driveway. It was mostly dirt with a few stray pieces of gravel, two deeply rutted tracks and weeds growing along the centre. The ruts were filled with water, left over from yesterday's storm. It had rained the last few days. It seemed like it was always raining since we moved here. Looking down I saw some footprints in the mud, leading away from the house towards the road. I realized they were made by Nicholas and I yesterday when we were leaving.

"This would be a pretty bumpy ride in a car," I noted.

"It would be really neat on a dirt bike, I bet," Nicholas responded.

The mud was still soft and we sank into it a little as we walked. I was grateful I'd worn my hightops today. I tried to walk around the puddles and avoid the worst patches of mud. I put my foot down into one of the tracks we'd made the other day and found that by walking in our old footprints I didn't sink quite as deep. I moved along to the next foot print and then the next, my eyes trained on the ground. Nicholas had moved ahead of me. He wasn't concerned about where he walked and happily stomped through the mud and water.

I stopped short and stared at the ground. "Nicholas, what's this?"

He turned around. "What is what?"

"This. The foot print in the mud."

He plowed back through the puddles, splashing water into my face.

"Nicholas you jerk!" I screamed as I wiped my face with my arm.

"Sorry. Where's the foot print?"

"Here," I said, pointing to the ground. It was now half filled with water.

Nicholas bent down to look more closely. I bent down

as well.

"What do you think?" I asked.

"I can't be certain...but I think...that maybe...it's an animal track."

"I know that! What kind of animal?" I screamed.

"How should I know? It's an animal, maybe a dog."

"But look how big it is!"

"A big dog. Come on let's get going. I need a muffin," he said as he straightened up and started walking again.

I put my hand down, just above the muddy water that filled the paw print. I stretched out my fingers. There was still space on all sides between the ends of my fingers and the edges of the track.

"Nicholas this isn't a dog!" I yelled, looking up to see him just a few feet farther along, crouched down. I stood up and moved quickly to his side.

He looked up at me. "More tracks. Here, coming from down the path. It's not a dog."

"I know, I just said that. The tracks are too big. Maybe it's like a bear."

"It's not a bear either," he stated.

"How do you know?"

"If it was a dog or a bear there'd be claws at the edges of the footprints. Dogs and bears always have their claws out," he said quietly.

"How do you know that?"

"I was a Boy Scout."

"If it's not a dog or a bear then what is it?"

"Something big, something that either doesn't have claws or can pull in its claws...like a cat."

"Like a tiger," I said under my breath.

"Yeah, like a tiger," Nicholas confirmed. He stood up and wiped his muddy hands on his pants.

"Nicholas, don't do that!"

"Sorry," he answered.

"Maybe Mr. McCurdy was out taking Buddha for a walk," I suggested.

"I don't think so. Maybe he was riding it," Nick said.

"Riding it? What are you talking about? He wouldn't ride on his tiger!" I exclaimed.

"Yeah, you're right, but you'll notice there's no other tracks out here besides ours and the tigers. So if he wasn't riding it, then Buddha is out here by himself."

"We have to get out of here."

"We can't go back the way we came," Nicholas said. "The tracks are leading out towards the road."

"But that doesn't mean it didn't double back into the bushes. We don't have much choice," I said. "Let's get to the house right away. Once we're with Mr. McCurdy we'll be okay."

"Sounds good to me. Let's run."

"No!" I said forcefully, and then lowered my voice to continue. "We should move slowly and quietly. Buddha might be sitting just over the bank or maybe he's watching us right now. If we run he might decide to chase us."

"We'll just outrun him then," he suggested.

"It can move faster than a racehorse. What makes you think you can move that fast? You're not even that good a runner."

"Believe me, if a tiger is chasing me I can become a good runner. Besides, Buddha wouldn't hurt me, I've fed him right from my hand."

"Good, now he thinks of you and he thinks of food. Since you don't have any food in your hand maybe he'd think of your hand as food."

That shut Nicholas up. We moved up the driveway, slowly, quietly, hardly daring to breathe. I looked apprehensively at the tall weeds and bushes and trees lining the lane way; any of these could offer the perfect hiding spot from which a tiger could pounce. I looked over my shoulder, gazing down the lane. No sight of anything. Turning back around I caught my first glimpse of the roof of the house. We rounded a small curve and then climbed an incline and the house was right ahead of us across a patch of grass.

"We're going to be okay," I said, more to myself than to Nicholas.

"This is one time I hope you're right."

Moving across the grass I was both reassured and unnerved. Reassured because there was no place for a tiger to hide but unnerved because we seemed so exposed.

"HEY MR. McCURDY!" Nicholas yelled.

I jumped straight up into the air, and then, without thinking I reached over and clipped him on the side of the head.

"What's the big idea! I was calling Mr. McCurdy."

"He could be anywhere," I replied.

"He could be anywhere, but he is right there," Nicholas answered.

"Where? I asked as I trained my eyes on the house. The sun was directly over the house and I squinted to see more clearly. "I don't see him."

"He's right there, sitting in a chair by the back door. Are you blind or what?"

I cupped one hand over my eyes and squinted harder. "Yeah, I think I see him. Why isn't he moving?"

"I guess he doesn't see us because the sun is in his eyes," Nicholas offered.

"The sun is in our eyes. It's behind his back and he's in the shade," I explained. "Anyway, he should have heard you yell."

"He's old and probably a little deaf," my brother countered.

"He didn't seem deaf to me."

As we continued to walk closer I could clearly make out Mr. McCurdy, sitting in a chair, a blanket draped over his shoulders, the end of his gun, resting on his lap and poking out from the blanket. He wasn't moving...at all.

"Must be asleep," Nicholas said.

"But why would he be here in the first place and why would he be holding a gun?" I asked.

Nicholas didn't answer. My eyes were trained on him, sitting in the chair, not moving. I strained to see anything. A flick of a hand, a nod of the head or his chest going up and down. We stopped in our tracks a few yards away from Mr. McCurdy. Nicholas and I looked at each other. From my brother's expression I knew he was expecting me to do something.

"Mr. McCurdy?" I said quietly.

There was no answer. No movement.

"Try it louder," Nicholas said, his voice barely above a whisper.

"Mr. McCurdy!" I stated more forcefully. There was no change. I thought I could see his chest move, ever so slightly, but I knew I couldn't trust my judgment.

"Nicholas...do you think he's D...E...A...D?"

"Dead? How would I know? Nana was the first dead person I ever saw. And why did you spell it, anyway?"

"I don't know, I just thought it was, I don't know, more polite."

"If he's dead it doesn't matter, and if he's alive I bet he can spell. Give him a shake," Nicholas said as he pushed me forward.

I moved on tiptoes until I stood right over him. His head was slumped down on his chest and I still couldn't tell if he was breathing beneath the blanket. Holding the muffin tray with one hand I bent over and took the other hand and gently touched his shoulder.

"Mr. McCurdy..."

"WHAT DO YOU WANT!?" Mr. McCurdy screamed as he lept to his feet. He knocked me backwards and the tray of muffins flew into the air as I slumped to the muddy ground and the muffins landed all around me.

"WHAT? WHAT? Oh it's just you two," Mr. McCurdy exclaimed as he stared down at me. "What are you doing sneaking up on a fella?"

"We weren't sneaking up. We came to visit. We brought you some muffins," I stuttered.

"Muffins?"

"Yes, muffins. They're right there," I said, pointing to the ground.

"They look mighty tasty," Mr. McCurdy said.

"They are," Nicholas chipped in, talking through a full mouth.

"But how did you...?"

"Caught it, mid-flight. Told you I'd get one," he said as he popped the last corner into his already-stuffed mouth.

"Nicholas Eric Fraser you are just such a...."

"This isn't the time, Sarah," he interrupted. "Don't forget the tiger."

"The tiger! That's right. Mr. McCurdy, Buddha is loose!" I said as I pulled myself to my feet.

"Don't be silly, Sarah, old Buddha's all tucked in. I just checked his cage."

"But we saw tracks," I protested.

"Probably a big dog," he stated.

"No claws," Nicholas mumbled, swallowing hard to clear away the last of the muffin.

"No claws?" Mr. McCurdy asked.

"There are no claw marks, just gigantic paw prints."

"Where? Where did you see them?"

"In the lane leading up from the road," I answered.

"Impossible, I've been here all night watching the lane and I didn't see anything."

"But you were asleep when we came up," I noted.

"Asleep? No, I was just resting my eyes for a few seconds."

"But why were you sitting there all night anyway?" Nicholas asked.

"Some darn fool kids were here last night. I heard them coming up the driveway and chased them away. Sat here all night to make sure they weren't coming back. Nobody came back. I scared them away, good."

We stood there in silence. My brother bent down, grabbed the tray and started gathering up the fallen muffins. He rubbed one against his pant leg and then took a big bite.

I gave him a disapproving look.

"Wanna bite?" he asked, offering me what remained of the muffin.

"They still look good to me," Mr. McCurdy chipped in. "Let's go inside. I betcha Calvin will want one too. That chimp has himself a real sweet tooth."

Mr. McCurdy walked over, pulled open the screen door and then froze in place. He turned to face me. "Maybe we should just go on down to the barn and see how old Buddha's doing. That would make you happy, wouldn't it Sarah?"

We walked around the side of the house and along the path leading to the barn. Nobody said a word. For Nicholas that would have been difficult if he wasn't stuffing his third, or fourth, muffin into his mouth. Coming up on the barn we circled around to the stable entrance. The door was open.

"I closed that door last night," Mr. McCurdy said, his voice breaking on the last word. He picked up his pace. Both Nicholas and I fell in behind him. I realized he wasn't carrying the rifle anymore. I guess he'd left it sitting on the chair, or leaning against the house.

He flung open the stable door. "Buddha, I'm coming to see ya boy!"

Nicholas and I came to the door and peeked into the darkened stable. At first I couldn't see anything. My brother gave me a small shove in the back and when I turned he motioned for me to enter. I took a few steps with him right on my heels. I saw Mr. McCurdy kneeling, motionless in front of the tiger's pen. I couldn't see Buddha. I moved closer until I was standing over him. The pen was empty and the door was ajar. I looked down at Mr. McCurdy. In his hand was a strand of thick chain.

"It's been cut," he said, showing me the chain, "right in the middle with some sort of hack saw. Didn't even touch the lock. See, it's still locked."

Mr. McCurdy rose to his feet, turned, brushed by me and started quickly walking back the way we came. "Show me the tracks!" he shouted over his shoulder.

We charged after him, this time wanting to keep up, but surprised by how fast he moved. There was no hint of his limp and he was practically jogging up the sloped path back towards the house and the driveway.

"Mr. McCurdy, Buddha's tame, right?" I asked apprehensively.

"He's as tame as a tiger can get," he answered without turning to look at me or breaking his pace.

"So he wouldn't hurt anybody, right?"

"I didn't say that. I said he's as tame as tiger can get, but that doesn't mean he's not a tiger."

"I don't understand."

"He may do what he's told, but he's still a tiger, he still thinks like a tiger and he still wants to act like a tiger."

He slowed down only when he reached the driveway.

"Show me!" he commanded.

We scrambled around searching for the tracks.

"Here's one!" I yelled.

Mr. McCurdy came over and dropped to his knees. Without saying a word he shook his head. On his hands and knees, he moved up the driveway until he came to another track and then another.

"Is it Buddha?" Nicholas asked.

"I hope so, because if it isn't then we've got ourselves two tigers on the loose right now," he answered. Mr. McCurdy stood up, his pants and hands covered in mud.

"What now?" I asked.

"There's only one thing we can do now," he answered quietly.

Chapter 5

"What?" Nicholas asked. "What do we do?"

"We go looking for him," Mr. McCurdy answered.

"But shouldn't we...call somebody?" By the time the words escaped my mouth Mr. McCurdy and Nicholas were gone. They were quickly moving up the drive, back toward the house. I sprinted after them. Falling in a half step behind, I heard Mr. McCurdy giving my brother orders.

"Go on back up to the barn. You'll find a heavy chain and a coil of rope hanging up on the wall just inside the stable door. Bring them back to the house."

"But what about the snake?" I questioned.

"No we don't need the snake. I don't see how he could help us," Mr. McCurdy replied.

"That wasn't what I meant!" I said with alarm.

"I know, I know. The snake won't hurt Nicholas." He turned to my brother. "You're not afraid are you?"

Nicholas laughed and then sprinted away to keep me from saying anything more.

"Shouldn't we call somebody?" I asked once again.

"Who'd you have in mind?"

"I don't know..." I said, letting the sentence hang unfinished.

"The dog catcher?"

We came to the house and Mr. McCurdy opened the screen door. "Grab that gun will you? We might need it."

Carefully I picked it up, holding it by the barrel, and followed him into the house. I was overwhelmed by the smell once again. I walked down the hallway to the kitchen. Mr. McCurdy was no where to be seen. Laura was there though. She was lying on her back under the kitchen table with her feet straight up in the air, tongue hanging out of her mouth, and eyes closed. As I watched, her eyes popped open. She stretched her legs and arched her back, then she righted herself and took to her feet. Her back was practically level with the bottom of the table and she rubbed herself against it, causing the legs of the table to slightly rise off the ground.

Even though I'd seen her every day for the last four days I really hadn't remembered how big she was. Maybe it was just because I was here by myself now, but she seemed to practically fill the room. She moved effortlessly and reminded me of a ballet dancer.

"Good Laura, nice Laura, gentle Laura," I said quietly. I wasn't sure if I believed what I was saying although of all the animals on the farm she scared me the least. But here alone with her, I didn't feel so brave anymore.

Mr. McCurdy burst back into the room. "Here, let me have the gun."

He took the gun from my hands and set it down on the counter. He opened up a box and placed it on the table beside the gun. He removed a series of glass bottles.

"AAAHH!" I screamed as I jumped backwards, to the accompanying sound of claws scraping against the linoleum floor as Laura scurried back across the floor and under the table, causing the bottles to shake.

"Don't scare my cheetah," Mr. McCurdy scolded me.

"*It* scared *me*! It was nibbling at my toes."

"Just means she likes you," he answered. "Come on over here."

I hesitated.

"Come on, don't worry about your toes, she's so scared of you now it could be months before she does that again. I need your help."

I moved over reluctantly, keeping one eye on Laura huddled under the table.

"Can you read this for me?" he asked.

"Can't you read?"

"Of course I can read!" he thundered. "But if you haven't noticed I'm an old man and this is real small writing."

"I'm sorry."

"Don't apologize, just read! No time to be wasting here."

I read the faded and yellowing labels of two of the bottles, not understanding any of the words I was reading until Mr. McCurdy called out, "That's the one!" He took a needle out of the box, the kind of needle they use to take blood, and dipped the end into the bottle. He drew back the handle and the needle filled with the liquid. Then he took the gun and opened the chamber to insert the needle.

"How about the police?" I asked.

"The police?"

"Yes. Shouldn't we call the police?"

"Be my guest," he said, motioning to the telephone on the wall.

I crossed the room and picked up the receiver. "Should I call 911?"

"You can dial anything ya want. It doesn't matter," he answered without looking over at me.

"What do you mean?"

"Phone doesn't work," he answered.

"Why not?"

"All I got was calls from people trying to clean my carpet or get me to subscribe to some newspaper or something, so I stopped paying the bill. Didn't seem like there was anybody I wanted to talk to anyway."

I was confused. "If it doesn't work, why did you tell me to call the police."

"Because it don't work."

"What?" I sputtered.

"I let you use the phone to call the police because I knew that you couldn't. If it had worked I wouldn't have let you. Only thing the police will do is keep me tied up here answering questions while they try to kill Buddha. We don't have time for the police."

I heard the screen door slam shut and then Nicholas appeared, a coil of rope around his neck and a chain in his hands, dragging on the ground.

"I better get my glasses. Sarah, can you go ever there and get me that box off the top of the fridge?"

I stretched up and grabbed the carton. Pulling it down I looked inside the open top. It was filled with dozens and dozens of pairs of eye glasses. I brought it over and placed it on the table in front of him. Mr. McCurdy reached in and pulled out a pair of glasses, putting them on. I watched as his eyes widened behind the thick lenses and he craned his head to one side.

"Nope, these aren't right," he said as he removed them. He dropped them back into the box and picked out another pair.

"These glasses can't all be yours?" I asked incredulously.

"Of course they are. Paid five dollars for the whole box at a flea market, a few years ago."

"I mean they all can't be, you know, the right lenses for you."

He put the second pair back in the box and reached for another pair.

"Of course they all aren't right for everything, but one pair helps me read, another helps me see far away and another pair is good for driving...."

"Then why don't you throw away all the others?" I interrupted.

"I never throw anything away. Never can tell when you might need something. Ahh, here they are!" he said. He removed a pair of pink ladies' glasses with rhinestones on the corners. He put them on. Nicholas started to laugh.

"Doesn't matter if they're good looking, as long as they help me look good," Mr. McCurdy chuckled. "You old enough to drive?" he asked.

"Me?"

"Who else?"

"I don't know how to drive. I'm only thirteen."

"I can drive," Nicholas announced.

"You! You're not big enough to see over the dash!" Mr. McCurdy laughed. "I guess *I'll* have to drive."

"Shoot!" my brother responded. "I don't get to do any of the really fun stuff."

"We'll help you put everything in your car, but then we better get going home," I said.

"Home?" both Nicholas and Mr. McCurdy said in chorus.

"Yes, home. Mom wouldn't give us permission to go along."

"You're right and that's why nobody is asking her for her permission. I don't see Mom anywhere around here," Nicholas said.

"I'm in charge and we're heading home. I hope you understand, but we just can't go. Can you drop us off, Mr. McCurdy?" I asked.

"I don't have time to be a taxi. Every minute I waste is a minute things can go wrong. I'm pretty sure Buddha headed the other way. You'll have to walk."

"Okay, then we better get started. Come on, Nicholas," I said as I brushed by him and started down the hall. I stopped and turned around. He wasn't following me.

"Nicholas...."

"Hold on a second. I want to ask Mr. McCurdy a couple of questions, okay?"

"Fine," I replied.

"Mr. McCurdy, can you be one hundred percent sure that Buddha headed toward town and not our farm?"

"I'm certain he's headed for town."

"But are you one hundred percent sure? Sure he didn't head the other way? The way Sarah and I are going to walk?"

"I can't be guaranteeing anything, but I'm pretty sure he's going the other way."

"And Mr. McCurdy, where is the safest place somebody could be if they ran into Buddha?" Nicholas asked.

"I don't quite understand what you're asking, but I guess in a house or a car."

"Or with you," Nicholas interrupted.

"Oh, sure, with me."

"And one more question. I know Buddha's probably headed in the opposite direction from Sarah and I, but if we should happen to run into him, do you think he'd hurt us?"

"I don't think so. Just make sure you don't go turning your back on him. Even I don't ever turn my back on him."

"Why not?" I asked.

"Like I said earlier, he may be trained, but he's still a tiger. That's how tigers kill. They jump you from behind.. With Buddha he'd just be playing, but when an eight-hundred-pound tiger plays with you, sometimes things happen."

"Sarah, I know Mom would be worried, but I also know she's always believed in helping people who need help and Mr. McCurdy needs our help. We should go along. We'll stay in the background, maybe even in the car if things get rough," Nicholas suggested.

"I don't know," I answered.

"We'd be helping, we'd be with Mr. McCurdy and we can stay safe in the car. What could be better than that?"

I knew when I was being conned, but most of what he said made sense. The thought of walking home, just Nicholas and I, and meeting up with Buddha, sent a shiver up and down my spine.

"Could we stay in the car?" I asked.

"If ya want," Mr. McCurdy offered. "I really would appreciate your help. I could use the extra pairs of hands."

"Please Sarah," Nicholas pleaded.

"I...guess it would be okay, but you have to listen to me. Okay?"

"No problem-o," my brother answered. "When do I ever not listen to you?"

"We don't have enough time for me to answer that question."

"Time's a wasting," Mr. McCurdy stated. He walked over to the doorway leading to the living room. "CALVIN! Come on CALVIN! Shake a leg, we've got to get moving!"

"Calvin? You're bringing the chimp?" I questioned.

"Have to. We may need the muscle. Maybe we'll have to move Buddha or even pick him up. Calvin is old but he's still as strong as three or four men," he explained.

As if on cue, Calvin came walking into the room.

"That's a boy, Calvin, we're going for a car ride," Mr. McCurdy announced.

Calvin shrieked loudly and I jumped straight up into the air in shock.

"Calvin loves a good car ride," Mr. McCurdy said.

Mr. McCurdy led the way, followed closely by my brother and Calvin. I followed reluctantly. The garage sat just off to the side of the house. Mr. McCurdy swung open the door revealing the rear bumper of an enormous car.

"Climb on in."

"It's a convertible," I said in disbelief.

"Yep. It's a nineteen sixty-five Lincoln Continental rag

top," he said proudly.

"But you said I could wait in the car when we find the tiger."

"Course you can."

"But it's a convertible," I said in confusion.

"Course it is."

"But how would that protect me from the tiger?"

"Protection? Why would you need protection? Buddha won't hurt you. Not with me around. Climb aboard."

Without bothering to use the doors, both Nicholas and Calvin climbed into the car, Nicholas in the back seat and Calvin in the front. Mr. McCurdy climbed in behind the wheel and I opened the driver's side back door and took a seat.

"No way, ape. Get into the back seat," Mr. McCurdy ordered. Reluctantly the chimp climbed over the seat and settled in partially between, and partially on top of, Nicholas and I.

"Hey, get off me!" my brother yelled.

"How about if one of you comes up here in the front," Mr. McCurdy suggested.

"Sounds good to me," Nicholas said as he scaled the seat before I could react. "Why didn't you want Calvin up here?"

"Stupid monkey is always playing with the radio. Besides, sometimes he gets car sick." He turned the key and the car roared to life.

"Car sick?" I echoed ominously.

"Yep. Car sick. Throws up."

I looked over at Calvin. He flashed me a grin. Great, just what I needed to make a bad day even worse; ape barf. I squeezed myself against the door, as far away from Calvin as

I could get.

Suddenly the car lept backwards and I was thrown against the back of the front seat. I pushed myself into place as the car swung out and then rocketed forward.

"Where are the seat belts!" I yelled over the roar of the engine and the rush of the wind.

"No seat belts. Classics like this were made before seat belts were ever installed in cars."

I braced myself in anticipation of the bumps and ruts of the driveway. Even with that, I was air borne, landing and bouncing and then launched skyward again.

"Hang on," Mr. McCurdy yelled.

Almost instantly I felt myself being thrown forward. A hairy arm reached out and held me in place as the car braked to a stop at the end of the driveway. The nose of the car was just out on the road. Calvin loosened his grip.

"Thank you," I said.

He took his hand and patted me on the top of my head. Mr. McCurdy got out of the car and circled around to the passenger side of the vehicle.

"I thought so. Do you smell it?"

"I smell something. What is it?" Nicholas asked.

"Chicken. The wind is blowing in from the chicken plant just outside of town. That's where Buddha's heading to."

"How can you be so sure?" I asked.

"Two things you have to know about tigers; first, they think with their stomach, and second, their nose is eight times as good as a person's, so that nose leads their stomach right to where the food is. That's where he's heading."

Mr. McCurdy came back into the car. "Sarah, when we're

driving I want you to keep your eyes peeled on the ditch on your side of the car. Nicholas you do the same on the other side."

Before I could answer the engine roared and the car jolted forward. The wheels whizzed on the mud of the driveway, propelling us forward until they caught the gravel of the road and stones went flying, hitting the undercarriage. The car swayed back and forth and I bounced sideways a couple of times between Calvin and the door.

I looked over at Calvin. He looked at me, puckered his lips and blew me a kiss. This wasn't really happening. I was in the back seat of an old convertible. I was sharing my seat with a chimpanzee. My brother was in the front, a coil of rope around his neck, fiddling with the radio. Our driver was a little old man, so small that he was looking through the steering wheel to see through the windshield. He was wearing a pair of funny woman's glasses and there was a loaded tranquilizer gun on the seat beside him. We were going hunting for a missing tiger. I couldn't wait until the first day of school when the teacher asked us to write about what we did on our summer vacation.

Between the roar of the radio and the wind rushing by the open roof, there really wasn't much chance for conversation. That was okay with me. I couldn't think of anything to say that would make any sense and besides all my attention was focused on the side of the road, searching for the tiger. It was a strange feeling. Part of me wanted to find Buddha and make sure he was okay. The other part, the biggest part, the truly wimpy part, hoped I never saw that tiger again.

I knew without asking that my brother didn't feel that

way. For him this was a big adventure. He didn't have to think about all the bad things that could happen; that was my job.

What I also had noticed was the change in Mr. McCurdy. True, I'd only known him for a few days, but today he seemed so much more 'alive'. He wasn't coughing, or limping, and his eyes were sparkly and bright. It seemed as if he was having the time of his life. It didn't much matter though. What chance did we have of finding the tiger anyway?

The car slowed suddenly. I took my eyes off the ditch and looked forward. There was a police car, lights flashing, blocking the road up ahead. A policeman stood in front of the car and waved his arms. Mr. McCurdy brought the car to a stop in front of the patrol car and the policeman walked toward us.

"I think we found our tiger," Mr. McCurdy said quietly.

Chapter 6

"Sorry for the inconvenience, but I'm afraid you folks will have to turn back," the officer said.

"No can do!" Mr. McCurdy announced.

"No choice, sir," the officer said with more than a hint of annoyance. "We have a...a...situation."

"I've never heard of a tiger being called a 'situation'," Mr. McCurdy replied.

"You know about the tiger?" the officer asked in surprise. "Regardless, I'm not to let any civilians past this point."

"Fine, no problem. We'll turn our car around and head back home. Of course, you'll have another situation to deal with when who ever is in charge finds out that you wouldn't let through the experts who were called in to deal with the problem." Mr. McCurdy started to put the car in gear.

"WAIT!" the policeman ordered. There was panic in his voice. "You mean you were called to deal with the tiger?"

"Didn't I just say that? Don't you know who I am?"

"Um, I'm afraid not, sir," he answered quietly, looking down at the ground.

"I'm Professor Angus J. McCurdy of the Institute for Animal Studies."

"Didn't you recognize him from his pictures or books?" Nicholas asked. He turned around and gave me a sly smile. It was amazing how well he could come up with a lie.

"No sir, I mean Professor, I didn't. Please accept my apologies."

"No apology necessary, officer, just aim us at the tiger."

"Yes, professor, just drive straight ahead. Its not far from here. The tiger is trapped in a barn. There'll be an officer in front of the house, by the road. He can direct you. If he tries to stop you, just tell him you've been cleared."

"Fine. You've been very helpful, Officer...?"

"Sinopoli, Frank Sinopoli," the officer said, pointing to the name tag on his uniform.

"Thank you. I'll be sure to pass on to your Chief just how helpful you've been."

"Thank you very much professor," the officer beamed.

"Do you know if anyone has been hurt by the tiger?" Mr. McCurdy asked.

"Thank goodness, no. The tiger was sneaking up on two small children playing in their yard when their mother went out to hang laundry. She grabbed the kids and somehow got them into the house and called us."

"And Officer Sinopoli, is the tiger okay?" Mr. McCurdy asked.

"Yes. He's okay, I guess. Nobody wants to get too close to find out."

"That's why they called us."

"Could I ask you a question, Professor?"

"Sure thing, but make it quick.

"I was wondering why you have a monkey with you?" he asked.

"My mother insisted that my sister come along with us," Nicholas answered.

Mr. McCurdy, Calvin and the officer all joined together in a chorus of laughter at my expense. I just slumped down lower in my seat.

"Oh you mean the other monkey," my brother said.

"Calvin has been specially trained for these situations. He deals with the most dangerous animals so no human life is at risk," Mr. McCurdy answered.

"Oh, I see, that's very interesting. Again, I'm sorry for the delay. Please proceed," Officer Sinopoli said.

Mr. McCurdy put the car in gear and steered into the empty oncoming lane of traffic to move around the patrol car. As we passed by, Calvin stood up on the back seat and blew another kiss, this time at the officer. I didn't dare look at the officer's reaction.

I leaned over the front seat. "I didn't know you were a Professor?"

"Ah, Sarah. He was lying," Nicholas said.

"I don't like to think of it as lying. I just think we're putting on a little performance. That's all a circus is, a performance. I need you two to just play along with whatever I say. Just like Nicholas did. Do you think you can do that Sarah?"

"I'm not sure."

"Let's play it safe. Sarah, just smile and nod," Nicholas said.

"Could I make one suggestion?" I asked.

"Sure thing, Sarah."

"Before we start talking to the any more police officers you should take off your glasses."

"Oh, that's a good point," Mr. McCurdy replied. He started to take them off.

"NO!" I yelled. "Wait until we stop driving!"

"Another good point," he agreed.

We didn't have to drive much further. Quickly we came to the house where Buddha was hiding. There were two more patrol cars angled on the road, one partly up on the sidewalk, and three more on the lawn, all with their lights flashing. As we pulled up to a stop, two more officers moved to our vehicle. They were both carrying shotguns. Mr. McCurdy turned the car off, pulled off his glasses, put them in his pocket, and opened his door before they had a chance to move too far forward.

"Stop! You can't come in here!" one of the officers bellowed.

"I don't have time to explain this to every blue uniform around here. Radio Sinopoli and he'll explain it. Any more delays and I'll make sure you two are directly responsible for anything that happens here!"

"But..." one of the officer started to say.

"I'll go and radio," the other offered and walked back toward his car.

"Good, good. Now while he's calling I need you to lead me to the where the tiger is hiding," Mr. McCurdy said to the other officer.

The officer didn't move.

"Do you want us to bring all the equipment, Professor?" Nicholas asked.

"Yes, please bring the special harness. Sarah, bring along

the extra medication and I'll carry the tranquilizer gun." He then turned specifically to the officer. "And you, turn those darn lights off."

"I can't do that," he protested.

"I'm telling you that you better turn off those lights or you might get that tiger all nervous and edgy and then he might just jump you."

"You can't tell me what to do," he said firmly.

"Do what he says," said the other officer, emerging from his squad car. "He's a world famous authority on tigers. He's been called in by the Chief. Do what he says."

"Says who?" the first officer questioned.

"Sinopoli gave me the low down. He must've been talking to the Chief. You turn off the lights on the cars and I'll lead them to the Captain."

We trailed after him up the driveway.

"They're lucky you just got back from your tiger study in Africa," Nicholas said so the policeman could overhear him.

"Africa?" the officer questioned.

"He meant India. My brother isn't very good at geography."

"Oh," the officer responded.

We continued to walk. The house was separated from the road by a rolling green lawn with a smattering of trees and shrubs. There was a swing set, where the kids probably were playing, a clothes line and an overturned laundry basket. We walked beside the house and I could see the barn. All around it there was a dozen or so officers. They all had shotguns or revolvers in their hands, and they were crouched behind trees or bushes. Their eyes were focused on the barn and we approached unnoticed. As we got closer the officer crouched down low and motioned for us to do the same. We followed his example, although it didn't make any sense.

"What does he think the tiger is going to do, take a shot at us?" Nicholas whispered.

In spite of myself I laughed and both Mr. McCurdy and the officer turned around. The officer shot me a dirty look. He led us to a small huddle of blue uniforms hiding behind a low hedge.

"Sir, the tiger experts have arrived," our escort announced to one of the officers.

He turned and looked at the officer and then at us. His eyes grew and his mouth dropped so far that if he'd been crouched any lower it would have brushed the ground.

"The what?"

"The tiger experts, Captain, sir," he repeated.

"Have you lost your senses completely? Get them out of here!"

"It's orders, sir, right from the Chief. We're supposed to follow his directions to the letter sir," the officer said nervously. This story was getting better with each officer who passed it along.

"You must be joking," the Captain replied, shaking his head.

"No sir."

"The Chief has given some crazy orders but this..."

"Would you like me to mention that to the Chief the next time he's over for a barbecue?" Mr. McCurdy said.

"NO!" the Captain said. "I mean, that won't be necessary."

"Sure thing. I want you to get all your men and have them fall further back. I need a little space to work," Mr. McCurdy answered.

"Do you want us to stay close enough to take a shot?" the officer asked.

"No, nobody is to take a shot. With the guns you have all you'd do is wound it and make it mad. If you think a tiger is dangerous you've never seen a wounded tiger. Just fall back."

"If our guns won't take it down, what are you going to do with that little gun of yours?" the Captain asked.

"It's not the gun, it's the bullet." Mr. McCurdy opened up the chamber and tilted the gun so the Captain could see the needle inside. "This is filled with a special medication just for tigers. One shot of this in its butt and it'll be as gentle as a kitten. I'll walk right up to him, slip a line around his neck and lead him away."

"Amazing!" the Captain stated.

"Yep, science is pretty amazing," Nicholas agreed.

The Captain gazed at Nicholas. He gave an order to one of his officers to have everybody fall back, but kept his eyes on us. He had a way of looking at you that would make you nervous even when you weren't doing one single thing wrong. And I did feel nervous because we were doing everything wrong. I just hoped when we got thrown in jail I didn't have to share a cell with my brother...or the chimpanzee.

"And who are these children and why are they here?" the Captain demanded.

"These are my grandchildren and they're here to help. Do you know anything about tigers?"

"Um...no...not much," the Captain admitted.

"Well these two know all there is to know and I need their help."

"Regardless of how much they know I'm afraid I must insist the children stay here. I can't jeopardize their safety," the Captain explained.

"They can stay here, at least until I get the shot at the cat. Then I'll need them. Do you want the ape to stay with you as well?" Mr. McCurdy asked.

"Ah, no, I guess the ape can go with you," the Captain agreed.

Calvin reached over and patted the Captain on the head. The other officers started to snicker, but stopped short when the Captain turned around and looked at them.

"Go now and take that ape with you," he hissed through clenched teeth.

"I need Nicholas and Sarah to come just a bit closer with the ape," Mr. McCurdy stated. "Don't you worry though, they'll stay back so they'll still be safe."

"Fine, whatever. Just keep them at a distance."

As we moved forward I saw all of the officers fall back. We'd only moved twenty feet when Mr. McCurdy motioned for us to stop.

"What are we supposed to do here?" Nicholas asked.

"Nothing. Just sit down here with Calvin and look like you're studying the situation," Mr. McCurdy said.

"Studying?"

"Yeah, studying. You remember, that thing you never do in school?" I taunted Nicholas.

"I just didn't want to leave you sitting there with the Captain. He asks too many questions. Wait here," Mr. McCurdy said.

As we watched, Mr. McCurdy started moving towards the barn. He crouched down low and walked in a zigzag pattern.

He stopped and pulled up a hand full of grass. He tossed it into the air so it got caught by the wind and blew back toward us. He turned around and gave us the thumbs up.

"What is he doing?" I asked.

"Probably just putting on a show. He can't just walk up and say hello to Buddha or people would know something was up."

Mr. McCurdy pushed the front door closed and then let the bar fall into place. He started circling around to the left side of the barn. As he passed by gaps in the boards he pressed his face against the building and peered inside. He turned the corner, and continued to do the same thing along the whole side of the barn, before disappearing around the back. Nicholas and I exchanged looks and waited for him to reappear.

Within half a minute he appeared around the corner and continued to peer through gaps and openings. He came back to the front door, turned back to where we were waiting, and motioned for us to come forward. Nicholas sprinted towards him. This was the opportunity he'd been waiting for. Calvin and I followed behind. Before we even arrived at Mr. McCurdy's side, my brother was heading around the back.

"Where is he going?" I asked nervously.

"Back of the barn."

"Why?"

"Because I told him to go there."

"But why?" I questioned.

"He's going to get Buddha's attention. Nicholas is going to go to the back and make a scrapping sound against the boards."

"How will that help?" I asked.

"When Buddha's head is pointed towards Nicholas, his back will be aimed at me. That way I can get in a shot. I want you to go and quietly open up the barn door, just a crack."

"Me? Why me?"

"Can't ask Calvin to do it. He's never done anything quietly in his whole life. Of course I could open the door and you could take the shot. Here, you want the rifle?" he said, offering it to me.

"No!"

"Okay, then you better get the door. And Sarah, as soon as I shoot, slam the door closed again."

I got up and moved toward the door. I took the bar with both hands and slid it out of the slot so the door could swing free. I heard a noise from inside the barn. I had to fight the urge to seal the door back up.

"It's just your brother," Mr. McCurdy whispered.

"How can you be so sure?" I whispered back.

"Because tigers don't make any noises. Open the door."

I took a deep breath and started to pull it open. My plan was to hide behind the door. Mr. McCurdy moved closer. He brought the rifle up to his shoulder and took aim. I held my breath and waited. Unexpectedly he lowered the gun. He reached into his pocket and pulled out his glasses. He put them on and then raised the rifle again. He peered into the barn and then brought the rifle up to his shoulder.

There was a "BAM", followed instantly by a "SWOOSH" and a "ROAR" from Buddha.

"Close the door!" Mr. McCurdy screamed. "Close the door!"

I threw myself against the door and slammed it shut. I

fumbled with the bar as I grabbed it off the ground and slid it into place.

Mr. McCurdy motioned toward the Captain for him to come closer. The Captain, followed by a group of officers, jogged towards us.

"In a couple of minutes I'll be going in and getting that tiger. I'll need you to get all your men farther away. The tiger will be dopey but I still don't want to get it all excited."

The Captain nodded his head to signal agreement and waved the officers off to follow his orders. As they left, Nicholas reappeared and came to our side.

"Well?" he asked.

"It worked," Mr. McCurdy answered. He looked at his watch. "All right, we've waited long enough. Captain, open the door. Nicholas, and Sarah, bring the lines and chain and wait at the entrance."

The Captain moved to the door and opened it. He handed Nicholas the gun and took the loop of rope from him. Mr. McCurdy entered and Nicholas tried to follow in, but I grabbed him by the arm and held him in place. Calvin squatted on the ground beside us and we all peered into the dark barn.

At first I couldn't see Buddha. I watched Mr. McCurdy move into the far corner and then caught sight of a tail. It was twitching, lashing back and forth. Mr. McCurdy talked quietly, but I couldn't make out any of the words. He moved up close to the stall where Buddha was hiding and then disappeared behind some boards. As I watched, the tail disappeared from view.

"Nicholas, maybe we should...."

I stopped mid-sentence as Mr. McCurdy came back into

view. In his one hand was a rope which trailed out behind him as he walked. My relief at seeing him was short lived as I caught sight of the tiger. I had to fight the urge to run.

"Wow!" Nicholas exclaimed.

As they continued to move toward us I saw the hypodermic needle sticking in Buddha's side. He moved calmly beside Mr. McCurdy. There was no strain in the rope which hung down, almost scraping the ground. Mr. McCurdy wasn't pulling the tiger, just walking beside it.

"Nicholas, bring me the chain."

My brother started forward, but I grabbed his arm again. He looked at me like I was crazy. "Don't worry, sis, it's drugged. Buddha's as gentle as a kitten." I released my grip and he strolled forward. I wasn't sure if he was really brave or just too dumb to be scared. He handed Mr. McCurdy the heavy chain.

"Here, hold this," Mr. McCurdy said, passing the rope to Nicholas.

Nicholas turned around and made a funny face. He didn't say a word but I was sure I knew what he was thinking: 'Look at me, I'm holding a tiger in one hand and a gun in the other!' I was thinking that Mom would have a heart attack if she was here to see this.

Mr. McCurdy fashioned a noose with the chain. He reached underneath Buddha's neck and hooked it over his head. Buddha shook and made a soft growling noise. Nicholas backed off and the rope became taut. Mr. McCurdy dropped the other end to the ground and started fumbling in his pockets. He pulled his hands out and stood holding his car keys.

"Here, Sarah, catch," he said as he lobbed them in my direction.

I reached up, they bounced off my finger tips and dropped to the ground. I bent down and picked them up.

"Give them to one of the officers and ask him to open up my trunk."

"Here, give them to me," the Captain said as he moved forward.

"And Captain," Mr. McCurdy called out. "Make sure everybody moves out of our way."

The Captain nodded in agreement and then disappeared out of the barn.

"Let's get moving, Nicholas. Come on, Buddha," Mr. McCurdy announced.

They started walking, the tiger in the middle, my brother holding onto the rope on one side and Mr. McCurdy holding the chain on the other. They were closing in on where Calvin and I stood.

"Should we move?" I asked nervously as I realized they had to practically walk through me to get to the door.

"You better. Sarah, come over and take a hold of the line your brother's holding."

"Are you sure it's safe?" I asked.

"It's just like walking a dog," Nicholas answered. "Come on, Sarah, don't be afraid."

I inched forward. Buddha seemed to be looking at me as I walked, his head slowly tilting to follow me as I moved. I tried not to look at him. Instead, I locked my eyes on Nicholas. I put him between Buddha and I, pushing him over slightly so that I could take the still coiled end. I played out a little more rope to give me another foot of distance.

"Calvin, come here!" Mr. McCurdy ordered.

Calvin rose to his feet and strode over to Mr. McCurdy. As he passed by he reached out one of his arms and gave Buddha a slap on the end of his nose. Buddha jumped back a few feet, squealing and Nicholas and I were almost pulled off our feet.

"CALVIN! Leave the tiger alone! Here, hold onto the chain."

Calvin took the chain. Mr. McCurdy dropped down on his knees and threw his arms around Buddha. He put his mouth directly beside one of Buddha's large ears. Once again he was talking. I couldn't make out the words. I could just tell the tone was soft and soothing. He released Buddha from the 'hug' and rose to his feet.

"All right, we better get moving. Nicholas, hand me the gun. I'll walk behind the tiger so it looks like I'm the guard."

We started walking. Calvin held the chain on one side, Nicholas and I held the rope on the other, Buddha between us, Mr. McCurdy behind us, with the now empty gun pointed at the tiger. Buddha moved slowly and calmly across the floor of the barn. As we came to the door we were pulled to a stop. Buddha had planted his feet and the rope was now taut. He didn't seem to want to leave the confines of the barn. I guess I really couldn't blame him, I wasn't so crazy about going out there either. There were police officers, lots of police officers, waiting just outside the door, armed and anxious.

"Get moving, old fella," Mr. McCurdy instructed Buddha as he gave him a slap on the rump. Buddha turned around, and snarled, but started moving.

"Everybody just keep calm. Move slowly, but keep moving. Don't worry about a thing."

Coming out of the barn I released one hand from the rope to shield my eyes from the sunlight. I scanned the scene and was relieved to find the nearest officer was quite a distance away. We strolled across the grass. I felt a trickle of sweat run down the side of my face and my hands felt slick and wet on the rope. Although Buddha wasn't pulling the line I'd tensed every muscle in my whole body, ready in case he decided to bolt. Thank goodness for the medication. If Buddha hadn't been drugged he could have dragged us around like rag dolls.

We rounded the house. I glanced over and saw a woman, an arm around two children, standing in the front window, watching. All three had their eyes wide open, following us as we walked across the front lawn. On both sides we were flanked by police officers. They seemed to be hidden behind every bush, tree and hedge along the route. There was even one, lying on his belly, hiding behind the laundry basket. Buddha didn't seem to see any of them, or maybe just didn't care. He glided along effortlessly. The only thing that was out of place was the needle, still stuck in his side, bobbing and bouncing along with each step he took. We came up to the cluster of patrol cars, sitting empty, all of their flashing lights now turned off. We moved between the last two cars. Both had their front doors open and we had to squeeze in close to Buddha to get by.

I had to smile as I saw Mr. McCurdy's car just up ahead. Just a few more steps and we'd be safe, or at least safer.

"Is Buddha going to sit up in the front seat?" I asked Mr. McCurdy.

"Nope."

"In the back seat with me!" I asked anxiously.

"Nope."

"But, what does that leave?" I asked.

"Why did you think I had them open up the trunk?"

"The trunk!" Nicholas and I exclaimed together.

"He's too big for the glove compartment," Mr. McCurdy chuckled.

"But we can't just put him into the trunk," I protested.

"It's specially made, that's where he always travels."

"Buddha would get all hot and—"

"SMILE EVERYBODY!" yelled a man with a camera as he jumped out from behind the caddy. A flash exploded. My eyes went starry and out of focus and I felt myself being pulled off my feet backwards. Instinctively I grabbed the rope tighter and felt myself being dragged backward. I closed my eyes. My ears were filled with the sound of running feet and loud voices.

"EVERYBODY STOP!" Mr. McCurdy yelled and then everything went quiet.

I opened one eye and then the other. I looked up and saw nothing but fur. Orange and black fur. I was lying on the ground, underneath Buddha. I closed my eyes again and went completely rigid.

"It's okay, just be calm," Mr. McCurdy said. I wasn't sure whether he was talking to me or to Buddha. Probably both.

"It's okay, Sarah, let me take the rope," Mr. McCurdy said gently.

I reached up both hands and I felt him take the rope.

"Now just get up, Sarah. Everything is fine, thanks to you."

I squiggled to one side and then rose to my knees. Mr. McCurdy was leading the tiger away. The chain was dragging on the ground behind him. Nicholas was sitting on the ground by the car. Calvin was in the back seat of one of the patrol cars, only the top of his head and his eyes peeking out. The police officers were much closer now. Two of them were leading away the man who had taken our picture. I heard him yelling about the "freedom of the press". A third officer followed behind carrying the camera. I watched as they brought the man over to a patrol car and placed him in the back seat.

I turned back to Mr. McCurdy and Buddha. Buddha followed obediently behind. They stopped at the rear bumper of the caddy.

"Come on, come on boy," he ordered.

Buddha hesitated for a second and then jumped up and into the open trunk. The car sagged and groaned under the weight. Mr. McCurdy leaned into the trunk as far as he could get without actually climbing in. Nicholas got to his feet and stood beside the trunk.

"Here, take this," Mr. McCurdy said as he handed my brother the heavy chain. Slowly Mr. McCurdy lowered the lid and then let it click closed. The Captain appeared from no where and vigorously shook Mr. McCurdy's hand. Other officers walked up, and surrounded Mr. McCurdy. He disappeared in the middle of a huddle of blue uniforms. Nicholas climbed into the front seat of the car. I felt a hand slip into one of mine and I looked up to see Calvin. He pulled on my arm and I was gently, but firmly, yanked to my feet. He held onto my hand and led me to the car.

I looked over the long trunk at the cluster of people. Mr. McCurdy finally emerged and rounded the side of the car. He climbed in and started it up. The crowd of officers parted and Mr. McCurdy slowly backed it up. Pulling free from the parked patrol cars he brought the car to a stop, changed gears and started it in motion forward. Suddenly the Captain was standing on the road, right in front of us, blocking the way, waving his arms. Mr. McCurdy stopped the car and the Captain strolled to the driver's side of the vehicle.

"Where can we get a hold of you?" the Captain asked.

"Why?"

"It's good to know, just in case we have another dangerous animal situation," he answered.

"Just ask the Chief," Mr. McCurdy answered. "We have to get the tiger into a cage before the medication wears off."

He put the car into drive and we started to move again.

We picked up speed quickly. I looked behind and was relieved to see the officers and their cars getting smaller and smaller. Turning forward I saw another patrol car coming towards us. In the few seconds between the time I could see the driver and the time that it passed, I recognized Officer Sinopoli. He waved hello.

"Sarah, can you pull down on that lever on the seat between you and Calvin, there," Mr. McCurdy asked.

"What's it for?"

"When you remove that section it lets light and fresh air into the trunk for Buddha."

I looked over and saw the handle. I pulled it and a small section of the back of the seat popped out, leaving a black hole that led into the trunk. I couldn't see Buddha. I couldn't see anything. Then as I watched I caught sight of motion and a large black nose pressed itself against the opening. Without waiting for permission I climbed over the seat and plopped down between Nicholas and Mr. McCurdy. They both chuckled, but I just ignored them. I looked back. Buddha had turned his head to the side and one enormous golden eye was staring out from the blackness. Then the eye vanished and was replaced by a large brown paw. It extended out of the hole and began 'fishing' around, seeing what it could touch. First the paw extended towards the empty seat where I had been sitting. Next it twisted and started to explore in the other direction. It inched towards where Calvin sat quietly. Suddenly Calvin reached out and gave the paw a slap. Like a rocket the paw was withdrawn back into the trunk. I gave Calvin the 'thumbs up' and he returned the gesture.

"How long before the shot wears off?" Nicholas asked.

That was a very good question, I thought. One that I wanted to know the answer to myself.

"Depends, but it's probably good for anywhere from four to six weeks," Mr. McCurdy answered.

"He'll be calm for six weeks!" I exclaimed.

"Longer than that. He's always calm. Haven't you two been listening to me. He's trained."

"But, how long will the shot last?" I asked again.

"I told you, from four to six weeks."

"But a tranquilizer can't last that long," I objected. "You said when you accidentally shot yourself that it only lasted for a few days."

"That's right. That's what happened when I shot myself with a tranquilizer. Maybe you do listen to some of what I say.

The thing is, I didn't give Buddha a tranquilizer."

"Then what did you give him?" I asked.

"A calcium shot."

"Calcium! Why did you give him a calcium shot?" I questioned.

"Because he needed it. You see, mainly all I can afford to feed him is chicken, so he needs a calcium supplement. About every month or so I have to give him a needle."

"But why did you give it to him today, with the gun, in front of the police?" I asked in confusion.

"Had to. If I hadn't shot him with a dart like I did, the police would have been suspicious that I wasn't an expert. Besides, didn't you feel a lot better thinking he'd been drugged?" Mr. McCurdy asked.

"So you tricked us," I stated.

"I think of it as protecting you. The calmer you are, the calmer the tiger is, and the calmer the tiger is, the safer you are," Mr. McCurdy reasoned.

"Makes sense," Nicholas said, nodding his head in agreement.

As we came to Mr. McCurdy's driveway he didn't slow down. We continued down the road in the direction of our farm. He slowed down the car and turned up our lane way.

"Don't you want us to help you get Buddha back into his cage?" Nicholas asked.

"I'll be okay, but thanks. Thanks, to both of you, for everything. I'm much obliged for all your help. If it wasn't for the two of you, that old tiger would be dead by now."

"That's okay. Thanks for the drive home," I replied.

We said our good-byes and climbed out of the car.

"In case you're interested I'll be home tomorrow if anybody wanted to drop on in, maybe with some muffins," he said smiling.

"Any special kind?" I asked, returning his smile.

"I'm partial to oatmeal, but the kind of muffins isn't nearly as important as the kind of people you share them with," he answered.

He drove away and we waved until the caddy disappeared from view. Nicholas and I walked into the house.

"Wait until we tell Mom what we did today!" Nicholas said.

"Are you crazy, we can't tell...." My sentence trailed off as I saw the big grin on his face and realized he was just putting me on.

"Just like eating pretzels, Sarah, just like pretzels," Nicholas said as he opened the door to the cupboard.

Chapter 7

"Good morning," my mother yawned, as she pushed through the swinging door and came into the kitchen.

"Morning," I grumbled.

"Certainly smells good. What's cooking?" she asked.

"Oatmeal muffins are baking in the oven and I'm making blueberry pancakes for breakfast," I answered without turning away from the stove.

"I hope Mr. McCurdy appreciates your baking."

"He does."

"Are you making enough pancakes for everybody?"

"Don't I always?" I flipped the four pancakes that filled the frying pan.

She stretched and yawned loudly. "I'm tired. It was late when I got in."

"No it wasn't. It was early. Early in the morning, like two thirty."

"It wasn't that late," she protested. "It was only two fifteen. I know because I woke Erin up to send her home and she left before two thirty. When did she put you to bed?"

"I don't get 'put to bed'," I said indignantly. "I went to bed at the regular time. I just couldn't sleep. I never can sleep until you get in."

"You've got to try. It's not fair to me to have to come home early when I'm on a date."

"Gee, I wouldn't want to be unfair to you," I muttered under my breath.

"What?" she asked.

"Nothing." I used the flipper to take the pancakes out of the pan and added them to the stack on a plate on top of the stove. I picked up the bowl of batter. I gave it a stir and some of the blueberries bobbed to the surface. I took a scoop and poured four more puddles of batter into the pan.

"Do we have any more of that real maple syrup?" Mom asked.

"Yes," I answered coldly, "we do."

"Sarah...don't be mad at me."

I felt her arms slip around me and she gave me a big hug. "Thank you for helping to keep things together." She turned me around. "It's good to know that I can always count on you. Reliable, dependable, Sarah."

I smiled. If only she knew. "Thanks."

"I wonder if the paper's arrived?" Mom asked. "I'll check."

As mom walked out one door, Nicholas walked in the other.

"Muffins?" he asked.

"Oatmeal muffins and blueberry pancakes," I answered.

"Can I have a muffin before we get there this time?"

"You can have a few. I baked an extra half dozen. But first, wash your hands."

I took the final batch of pancakes out of the frying pan and turned off the burner. Nicholas strolled to the kitchen sink and rinsed off his hands. Mom walked back into the kitchen, her face hidden behind the paper.

"Let's see what your horoscope is for today," she announced as she took a seat at the table.

"Mine first!"

"Okay. Nicky...hmmmm...Taurus, the bull."

"I always thought the bull part fit," I laughed as I opened the oven to remove the muffins.

"Exciting things are about to happen. Be prepared for an adventure," Mom read.

"Are you sure that isn't yesterday's paper?" Nicholas asked.

I shot him a dirty look.

"What?" Mom asked.

"Oh nothing. What does Sarah's say?" he asked.

"I don't believe in horoscopes," I said. "You always told me you didn't either, Mom."

"Things change. There's nothing wrong with a little fun."

"There's a difference between fun and..." I stopped short as I turned around to look at Mom. I couldn't see her behind the paper. All I could see was the front page of the paper and on that page was a large color photograph. I was too far away to make out the faces on the people, but I could clearly see a tiger. I closed my eyes and said a small, silent prayer; "Please, please, don't let that be us and Buddha."

"Now, my horoscope is interesting," Mom said. "'Surprising things will happen. These surprises will change the way you see people'. Interesting."

I moved closer, carrying the plate of pancakes. I could

now see clearly. There we were on the front page of the paper. I put the plate on the table. Nicholas reached for the pancakes and I grabbed his arm. He looked up. I pointed, dumbly, to the picture. His jaw dropped.

"What do you think about that, Sarah?" she asked.

I didn't answer. I didn't know what to say.

She lowered the paper, the picture folding up so I couldn't see it anymore.

"Sarah, what's wrong? You look like you've seen a ghost!" She turned to my brother. "Nicholas! You look the same!"

"We're just...hungry," he said.

"Yeah, hungry. Why don't you put down the paper so we can eat," I suggested.

"You're right. I shouldn't be looking at the paper when I could be looking at the two of you." She folded up the paper and put it down on the table. The picture was face down.

"Since Sarah made the pancakes, you and I should set the table, Mom."

"That's thoughtful of you Nicky. I'll get the plates while you get the cutlery and glasses."

"Do you think we could use Nana's plates?" my brother asked.

"Nana's plates?"

"Yeah. The ones in the dining room."

"That's a lot of work for now. Let's eat and we can use them for dinner," Mom suggested.

"Please, Mom. Sarah made us special blueberry pancakes. We should do something special too," Nicholas pleaded.

She smiled. "How can I say no when you ask so nicely. I'll go and get them." Mom rose from her seat. She pushed through the doorway to the dining room and the door swung shut behind her. Instantly Nicholas picked up the paper and sprinted across the length of the kitchen and out the other door. I ran after him. By the time I was through the door he was already upstairs. I caught up to him in his room.

"What does it say?" I asked.

"Read it for yourself," he answered.

I peeked in over his shoulder.

"ESCAPED TIGER RECAPTURED" read the headline.

"Mrs. Mollie Lahnsteiner thought she was seeing things when she went out to hang her laundry and saw a tiger stalking her two small children as they played in the backyard. Without thought for her own safety, she charged the full grown tiger and hit it with the laundry basket. The startled tiger ran for shelter in the family barn while Mrs. Lahnsteiner grabbed her two children, Brendan and Jordan, and retreated to the safety of the house, where she called police. Heavily armed police quickly sealed the area, trapping the beast in the barn.

Police contacted a world renowned tiger expert, reported to be Professor Angus McCurdy. Accompanied by two unnamed children and a chimpanzee, he arrived on the scene. Using a tranquilizer gun he subdued the tiger before leading it away to a specially constructed vehicle (story continued on page 2)."

"Wow!" I exclaimed quietly. "Wow!"

"Nice picture isn't it? Well at least I look okay. Your hair looks funny," Nicholas said.

"Are you crazy? Forget whether you look good!" I practically screamed. I grabbed the paper from his hands. "Come on, we have to get back down stairs. We have to tell Mom."

"Tell her! And you're calling me crazy? We can't tell her. She'll kill us," he yelled.

"What choice do we have? She'll see the front page of the paper and we'll be dead."

"I can just about guarantee that she'll never see this paper again," Nicholas replied.

"What good would that do? Somebody else will just see the picture and tell her about us."

"Yeah, our picture, but not our name. We're the 'unnamed children'," he said.

"Don't you understand? Our pictures are on the front page of the paper!"

"I know Sarah but nobody for two thousand miles around here knows who we are. Who do you think will recognize us?"

I thought about what he'd just said. "Well, what about Erin? She knows us."

"You're right, she does know us, but she doesn't know anything else. Do you really think Erin even reads the papers?" Nicholas asked.

"What's to stop Mom from getting another paper?"

"We won't let her leave the house," he answered.

"We can't keep her trapped here forever."

"We don't have to. Just for today. By tomorrow there'll be another paper with another picture on the front page and this one will be history."

"Do you really think we can get away with it?" I asked.

"We have to." He took the newspaper from my hand, crumpled it up into a ball and stuffed it under his bed. We raced back into the kitchen, but weren't in time to beat Mom back. She was setting the table with Nana's dishes.

"Where were you two?"

"Um...in the washroom," I lied.

"Both of you? At the same time?"

"We were washing our hands, you know, so we could eat," he added.

"Didn't you already wash your hands? Right there at the kitchen sink."

"Yeah but that was kitchen water. I wanted to use washroom water to wash with," he tried to explain.

"Nicholas there is no difference between the water in the kitchen and water...you were kidding...right?"

Nicholas smiled and sat down at the table. My Mom sat down beside him. I passed the plate of pancakes to my brother who passed them to Mom and then they circled back to me.

"Mom, do you think we could just hang around the house today?" he asked.

"I was thinking that maybe we could go into town and get groceries."

"Can't that wait until another day? Couldn't we just spend some time together, the three of us?" Nicholas asked.

"We'll see," Mom answered.

Nicholas broke into a smile. He'd told me that whenever Mom said 'we'll see' it meant it was a sure thing. I took a fork full of pancakes and stuffed them in my mouth. They weren't hot anymore, but they were still warm. Just as I went to pour on the maple syrup the phone rang.

"I'll get it," Nicholas yelled as he jumped to his feet.

Mom grabbed his arm. "Sit down. I jump for phones all week long. I want to sit and enjoy a breakfast with my two favorite people."

"But what if it's important?" Nicholas argued.

"Nothing's more important than this time together, just the three of us. Besides, the answering machine will pick it up."

Nicholas retook his seat. After the fourth ring we heard the machine click and spring to life in the other room. I listened to our greeting and then the beep. I half expected the person to hang up before the beep. I always did. I hated talking to a tape recorder.

"Ellen...."

I recognized the voice, it was my mother's sister, Aunt Elaine, calling long distance. She lived half a continent away.

"I couldn't believe it when I opened my paper and saw a picture of your children walking with a tiger. The picture made the wire services and apparently is on the front page of papers across the country. I know you moved to find new adventures, but this is unbelievable. Give me a call."

There was dead silence. Mom's face turned white, like all the blood was draining away.

"Could you pass the syrup," Nicholas asked.

Mom looked at him in disbelief. "What did you say?" she asked my brother.

"The syrup, could you pass it? It's right by your elbow."

"Is that all you can say?" she asked, her voice getting strained and pinched.

"Please?" he asked.

In a burst, the color returned to her face and it became beet red. She opened her mouth but no words came out. She pushed the plate of pancakes away from her slowly, and deliberately. Then she folded her hands in front of her. She glanced quickly around the kitchen.

"Where is the newspaper?" she asked quietly.

"What makes you think that we know—"

"NOW!" she yelled, interrupting Nicholas.

He popped up from his seat, and scurried out of the room, leaving me and Mom alone. I looked over at her. She gave me that look, that 'parent look', the one I hadn't seen for a long time. I looked away. We didn't have to wait long as Nicholas returned carrying an armful of paper. Mom straightened it out and then started sifting through the pages. She found the front page with the picture on it and pressed it flat so she could read the crinkled text. She looked at the picture and then looked up at me. Her eyes were widened in shock. She put her head back down to read the story. I watched her as her eyes moved back and forth across the page. She turned the page to read the 'continued' part.

"Good pancakes, Sarah," Nicholas said.

I glanced over at him in total disbelief. He was eating away like nothing was wrong.

"Explain this to me. How could this happen?" she asked.

"Nice picture isn't it?" Nicholas commented.

"Be quiet. Sarah explain this to me this instant! I want to know how you could let this happen. I leave you to care for your brother and you put both him and yourself at risk. I am disappointed in you. Very, very disappointed!"

"I'm sorry, " I started to say, but then stopped. "You're disappointed in me?"

"Yes, disappointed in you. I would expect something like this from your brother or even your father, but not from you."

"So," I swallowed hard. "So, if they did it, then it would

be okay?"

"Don't be silly, Sarah!" she replied with her voice getting louder. "It wouldn't be okay if anybody did what you two did."

"I am so sorry I disappointed you," I said, imitating my mother's voice. "It's so unlike anybody in this house to disappoint anybody else."

"Don't you talk to me like that!" she shrilled. "I expect you to be more responsible."

"Yeah, right," I answered under my breath. I was thinking about how 'responsible' it was for her to drag us half way across the country and turn our lives upside down.

"Don't talk to me with that tone of voice!" my mother ordered.

"I'm sorry, I just need to...." I got up and started walking away.

"Sarah! Come back here and sit down this instant! I'm not finished talking to you!" Mom yelled.

I thought about what she said, but turned and ran through the door, up the stairs and into my room where I buried my face in my pillow. I waited in my room, listening in silence. Part of me wanted her to leave me alone and the other part wanted her to come up and try to talk, but I knew she wouldn't be coming. My mother's way of dealing with any disagreement was to ignore it and hope it went away. One thing she said, though, was very right. I did need to talk. I just didn't need to talk to her.

I got up from my bed and moved across the room. There was no noise except for the creaking of the floor under my steps. Going down the stairs I could hear the TV. The door to my mother's office was closed which meant she was in there working. There was a chance she'd stay in there all day, only coming out for coffee. I moved across the kitchen, grabbed my coat off the hook and left the house.

As soon as I got out of sight of the house I went into the tall weeds that grew in the ditch. I knew she didn't know I was gone yet, but I wanted to make sure she couldn't find me if she went looking. I wasn't going to be found until I was good and ready to be found.

I climbed out of the ditch and went into the grove of trees. I moved aimlessly at first, just trying to get away. I had to make a big curve around to get to Mr. McCurdy's without walking too close to our house. There was a fallen log up ahead, blocking the path and I started to run faster to gain enough speed to leap over it. I jumped, but one foot caught on the very top of the fallen tree and I tripped, landing face first into the soft dirt on the other side. I stood up and dusted myself off. My left elbow hurt. I sat down on the log and rolled up my sleeve to check the damage. It looked fine.

As I sat there my mother's words came rolling back. My tongue felt thick and my bottom jaw was beginning to tremble. "I'm not going to cry," I said softly to myself. "I'm not going to cry." Before the last word was out of my mouth, the tears exploded.

I got up and started to walk again. I moved through the trees until I reached one of our fields. We'd rented it out to a neighboring farmer and he was growing corn. I moved between the rows, careful not to trample on the waist high plants. It would have been easier, and faster, to double back and go along the road, but there was no telling if my mother was out looking for me. I guess I'd have to stick to the cross country route although I'd never been on a short-cut in my life that didn't get me lost.

My father always tried to bring us along 'short-cuts'. We'd drive and drive, all the time Mom telling him that he was lost. He would say he knew exactly where he was going. She'd keep on trying to get him to stop for directions and he'd refuse. Mom said that something about him wouldn't allow him to ever admit he was lost, wrong, or to ask for directions.

I came to the fence marking the division between our place and Mr. McCurdy's. It wasn't really a fence, but more like a pile of rocks which had been taken out of the fields each spring over the last hundred years and just piled there to get them out of the way of the planting. I climbed awkwardly over the loose stones, a couple of the smaller ones moving underfoot. I was now on Mr. McCurdy's property.

I only had a rough idea of which way to head so I was relieved when, in the distance, I saw the weather vane at the top of his barn. I just aimed as best I could toward it, skirting around a pond and a thick patch of trees, but keeping it in sight. Since I was coming in from the back I'd have to pass by the barn. Part of me wanted to pop into the stable to say hello to Buddha, but the thought of the big snake lurking in there somewhere kept me going up to the house.

I walked up the gravel path and circled around the house. The chair was still sitting beside the door and I half expected Mr. McCurdy to be sitting in it. I pulled open the screen and knocked on the big wooden door. I heard sounds from inside. I imagined Laura scampering up the hall to see who was there. Then I heard Mr. McCurdy's voice, talking to his animals, and the door popped open.

"Sarah! Come on in, it's good to see...." His smile faded to a look of concern. "What's wrong, Sarah? You've been crying."

"Nothing's wrong," I started to say and then burst into tears. Mr. McCurdy put his arm around me and ushered me into the house. We walked down the hall and he sat me down at the kitchen table.

"How about a cup of tea? My mama always said bad things seem a little bit better over a hot cup."

"Yes, please."

As Mr. McCurdy walked across the kitchen to put the kettle on I felt something warm settle onto my lap. I looked down and there was Laura, looking up at me.

"Hi, Laura." I put a hand down to pet her on the top of the head. She responded by lifting her head and put her front paws on the chair so her head was level with mine. She pushed her nose right up against mine, opened her mouth, and licked me.

"Laura really does like you, Sarah. She doesn't usually take to new people."

"Neither do I," I replied as I scratched Laura behind the ear.

"Tell me what happened, tell me why you were crying."

"I don't want to talk about it."

"Don't be telling any lies, either to me or to yourself," Mr. McCurdy replied.

"What do you mean?"

"You want to talk."

"What makes you think I want to talk?" I questioned.

"Either you come to talk or I'm just so darn good looking you can't keep your eyes off me. I looked in the mirror this morning and I think I'm forty years past good looking," he chuckled as he sat down at one of the other chairs that circled the table.

I nodded my head in agreement. "I want to talk."

"That's better, now tell me what happened."

"My Mother found out about yesterday."

"She really must be mad at you."

"Really mad."

"And is that why you were crying?"

"Yes. I think...not really," I admitted.

Mr. McCurdy got up and walked over to the stove. He turned off the kettle just as a little trickle of steam was starting to escape from the spout.

"I just forgot that I'm out of tea. But don't you worry. We'll just go out and get some more. I was figuring that we could go and borrow some from my neighbour."

Instantly I understood what he meant. "I don't want to talk to her right now," I protested.

"No choice. Don't make me use the tranquilizer gun again," he said, fixing me with a steely gaze. "Come on, Sarah, I played a part in all of this so let me play a part in fixing it."

"But, I don't want...."

"Do you think we should bring Calvin along?" Mr. McCurdy interrupted. His face was completely solemn and then he broke out into a laughing fit. "Can you imagine the look on your mother's face when we come waltzing in with Calvin?"

I could just picture the chimp coming in, walking over to the fridge and rummaging around for a can of Coke while my mother climbed on top of the table. For somebody who'd been raised on a farm she was particularly afraid of animals, especially big animals. Between her fears and Dad's allergies, we'd never had a pet, not even a goldfish.

"If I was going back, I'd love to bring Calvin along, but there's no point in trying to talk right now. You don't know my mother. When she gets mad like this the best thing to do is just to leave her alone for a while. Later, maybe tomorrow, she'll be ready to talk."

"I can't force you, I guess. Besides, Calvin's still asleep and he's not much fun first thing in the morning. Your mama probably thinks the worst of me now, without bringing along a smelly, grumpy, old ape. Come on, let's get moving," Mr. McCurdy announced.

"But I said I'm not going to talk to her," I restated more forcefully.

"I know, I know. Remember, I'm old, but I'm not deaf. When you talk to her is something you have to decide for yourself. But, I've got to get into town to pick up a few things and I can't leave ya here by yourself. I really am out of tea. I'll drop you off on my way in."

"It's not on your way. My house is in the other direction," I said apprehensively, wondering if he was trying to talk me into something.

"I know which way town is, but I'll drop you off anyway. Your mom must be worried and I think you should at least be where she can see you even if she can't talk to you."

I gave him an uncertain look.

"Don't worry, Sarah, I'm not trying to fool you. I'll let you off at the end of the drive and turn right around. Okay?"

I nodded in agreement.

"You can sit up front if you promise not to play with the radio, or bring up," Mr. McCurdy offered.

"I promise."

We went to the garage and climbed into the car. He started it up and backed it out of the garage. He put it into gear and we started to move when I looked up and saw three police cars coming up the drive. My heart rose up into my throat. They came to a stop, blocking our way. The doors on all the cars opened and half a dozen policemen walked towards us.

In a rush, the feelings I'd felt yesterday, and I'd temporarily forgotten, came flowing back. I looked away from the approaching men to Mr. McCurdy. He didn't look scared. He looked almost amused.

"I hope they haven't come for tea," Mr. McCurdy said, "because I'm all out."

Chapter 8

The officers came up the driveway in a column. Leading the way was an older man in a fancy uniform. I had a sinking feeling that this was the "Chief." They filed around to the driver's side.

"You better move those cars, you're blocking my way and I've got someplace to go," Mr. McCurdy said.

"What did you say?" the older man thundered.

"I said you're blocking my way. Are you deaf?"

"Am I what?"

"DEAF!" Mr. McCurdy yelled.

"Don't you know who you're talking to? I'm the Chief of Police!" he bellowed.

"Good. Now I know who's blocking my driveway. Get those cars out of my way," Mr. McCurdy answered.

The Chief looked like he was going to scream. His nose was so big and red I thought it might explode. I looked away but noticed a couple of the officers grinning.

"Out of the car this instant!" the Chief roared.

"Why?" Mr. McCurdy asked. "I'm pretty comfy right here."

The redness from his nose spread across his whole face and down his neck until it disappeared beneath his uniform. He turned to face the men. "Get him out of the car, by force!"

Nobody moved.

At that instant another police car rolled up the driveway. It pulled off the drive so it could pass the parked cars and it came to an abrupt stop. The door opened and I recognized the Captain. Quickly he walked over to the Chief's side.

"I want this man dragged out of his car!" the Chief ordered.

"Can't do that, sir," the Captain replied calmly.

"Why not!"

"He's in his car on his property and he's done nothing wrong."

"What do you mean nothing wrong? He claimed he knew me, he said he was a tiger expert! He let an animal go that is a danger to public safety! What do you mean he did nothing wrong?"

As the Chief started yelling he moved closer and closer to the Captain until they were nose to nose. The Captain didn't budge an inch. His expression didn't even change although I could see little bits of spit flying out of the Chief's mouth and bouncing off the Captain's face.

"As I said, earlier, sir, Mr. McCurdy has not violated any sections of the Criminal Code," the Captain said as he wiped his face with the back of his sleeve. "Can you tell me under what section you propose that I arrest him?"

The Chief kicked his foot into the gravel, a spray of stones hitting the side of the car.

"Hey! Watch the paint job or I'll have *you* arrested," Mr. McCurdy barked.

All of the officers, including the Captain, smiled, and two started to chuckle. The Chief turned around and faced them and they all became silent and sober.

"That's enough from you! Fan out men, and let's find the tiger!" the Chief ordered.

Nobody moved again. The Captain walked up to him. "We can't, sir." I noticed how he spoke the word 'sir'. I think he felt the same way about taking orders from the Chief as I did taking orders from Erin.

"Why can't we?" he demanded.

"No search warrant or grounds for a search," he replied. "Can we talk in the car, sir?"

"Talk?" he asked in a confused voice.

"Yes, sir. Talk, sir. Please come with me," the Captain said calmly and then turned on his heels and walked back to one of the squad cars and the Chief followed. They both took a seat in the front seat of the car. Of course I couldn't hear what they were saying, but I watched in fascination. It started out with the chief waving his arms about and yelling. Slowly he seemed to settle down and then began to simply nod his head in agreement with whatever the Captain was saying. The Captain got out of the car, leaving the Chief sitting in the front passenger seat. The Captain then motioned for the other officers and they gathered around. They huddled around him and then, after a few seconds, scattered and moved back to their cars. One officer got in behind the wheel of the Chief's car. All of the cars, except for the one that the Captain had driven up in, juggled around and bounced down the driveway, leaving behind a cloud of dust. The Captain watched the other cars leave while he sat on the hood of his car, along with one other officer. The other guy was the first policeman we'd met yesterday, Officer Sinopoli. As the last car vanished down the driveway, the two of them strolled over to us.

"That Chief of yours is a strange old bird, isn't he?" Mr. McCurdy said.

The Captain and Officer Sinopoli exchanged a look. "The Chief has his own way of doing things. He's been with the force for over forty-five years. He'll be retiring next year," the Captain answered. "Can we go inside and talk, instead of standing in the driveway?"

"Sounds more like you want to visit than talk, but I think we can do that, as long as you don't want a cup of tea—we're out of that."

Mr. McCurdy turned the car off and we climbed out. We started walking to the house, the two officers trailing a dozen paces behind.

"What about Laura and Calvin?" I asked quietly.

"What about them?"

"Shouldn't you put them away, or warn the policemen about them being in the house?"

"They've already met Calvin, remember?"

"Yeah, but they don't know about Laura and besides they don't know that Calvin wanders free around your house," I reasoned.

"Good thinking, Sarah, but one of the only reasons I'm inviting them up to the house is to see their faces when Laura strolls over," he chuckled.

Arriving at the house, Mr. McCurdy opened the screen door, pushed open the inside door and then made a gesture for the two officers to enter. "Please," he said, and the two entered before us. Single file they moved up the narrow hallway.

"What the heck!" I heard the officer shout and knew he'd spotted Laura. There was a scrambling of feet as he quickly backed up and bumped into the Captain, nearly causing both of them to tumble over.

"Didn't think that two grown men, especially two police officers, would be scared of a little house cat," Mr. McCurdy stated as he gently squeezed by the two men. "Hi Laura," he said and the cheetah ran over, and rubbed against him, rising up onto her back legs.

I moved past the two officers as well. I looked back. "She's very gentle." I had to fight to keep the smile off my face.

"Come on in boys, take a load off your feet," Mr. McCurdy said, pulling out a chair from the table.

Both men moved cautiously across the floor, keeping one eye on Laura, who had retreated to her favourite place on the couch at the far side of the kitchen. They settled into two chairs. Mr. McCurdy occupied the third. In a burst of bravery I walked across the kitchen and sat down on the couch, beside Laura. I scratched behind her ears and she stretched out, and then snuggled her head into my lap. I looked over. All eyes were on me. Mr. McCurdy looked pleased while the two officers looked on with their mouths hanging open.

"Well, boys, what can I do for you?" Mr. McCurdy asked.

"I want to start by telling you what you did was wrong," the Captain said.

"What's so wrong with going to pick up my lost cat?"

"Please, let's not play games. People could have gotten hurt."

"That's what I was trying to make sure didn't happen."

"You should have been more honest with me about who you were and what was happening."

"Me, not honest? What did I say that wasn't honest?" Mr. McCurdy asked, looking completely innocent.

"You said you were from an animal institute."

"That's what I call my farm here, 'The Animal Institute'."

"How about you saying you were a 'professor'?" the Captain asked.

"That's my nick name. Lots of people have nicknames. Do you have one?"

"Yes, I have two...Captain and Sir."

"Aren't you going to question what I said about being a tiger expert?" Mr. McCurdy asked.

"No. That's one fact nobody could argue with, but you still should have been more truthful."

"Let me ask you a question, and I want an honest answer. If I was to have told you the truth would you have let me take my tiger home?"

The Captain didn't answer right away. "No, I probably wouldn't have."

"There you go. Sometimes you have to bend the truth a little to do the right thing," Mr. McCurdy crowed.

"I'm not happy with what went on."

"Would it make you happier if I put the tiger back?" Mr. McCurdy asked sarcastically.

"Of course not. That's what I really want to talk about. I want to know how it got away and to make sure that it doesn't happen again."

"It happened because of some fool teenagers. And, the

way to stop it from happening again is for you to do your job and arrest those kids," Mr. McCurdy said angrily.

"Do you know the names of those who are responsible?" the Captain asked.

"Of course not."

"Can you at least give us a description?" Officer Sinopoli asked.

"Baseball caps, jeans, smart alecks...like every teenager I've ever met. Teenagers are nothing but trouble, they...." He stopped abruptly and looked at me. "My apologies, Sarah, not all teenagers."

"How do you even know anybody freed the tiger? Maybe it got loose on its own," the Captain questioned.

"It's one smart tiger, but I don't think he knows how to use a hacksaw."

"Hacksaw?" Officer Sinopoli questioned.

"Somebody cut through a heavy chain," Mr. McCurdy replied.

"Regardless. You have to either safeguard the tiger, so this doesn't happen again, or find another place for the tiger to live," the Captain stated firmly.

"Someplace else? He's been with me since he was a kitten."

"Maybe you could let it go back into the wild," Officer Sinopoli suggested.

"Wild? Buddha's never been in the wild. He and his parents and their parents were all raised in captivity," Mr. McCurdy explained.

"It's not fair to the animal or to the community if that tiger gets out again. The next time things won't necessarily work out so well. Somebody might die. Think about him going to a zoo or a game park or something," the Captain reasoned.

"Why don't you just do your job and stop those boys from bothering Mr. McCurdy and his animals!" I snapped.

Everyone looked at me in shock and I must admit even I was shocked by my outburst. "You should put an officer up here to make sure those teenagers don't come back and bother Mr. McCurdy!"

"Sarah," the Captain said quietly, "you have to understand we can't do that. You can't expect me to post an officer up here every night, forever, can you?"

"I...I guess not," I answered meekly. "But what about for tonight, or the next few nights?"

"A few nights? What good would that do?" the Captain asked.

"He's right, Sarah, there's no guarantee they'll be back tonight. I get kids up here some nights and then they don't come back for weeks," Mr. McCurdy explained.

The Captain looked at Mr. McCurdy, long and hard. "I can't guarantee that nobody will come and bother your tiger, and it sounds like neither can you. If that's the case you have to find some place else for the tiger to live."

"Are you giving me an order?" Mr. McCurdy asked.

"No. You know that I have no authority to order you to do anything like that."

"Then I guess you'll want to be going now," Mr. McCurdy said.

The Captain motioned for Sinopoli to get up and they started down the hallway.

The Captain turned around. "You know that this isn't the end of it."

"Sounds like a threat," Mr. McCurdy said.

"I'm sorry if it sounded that way. I have to admire the way you handled yourself the other day, even if you did make me look like a fool, but I know that things aren't going to end here. Take good care of that tiger, and yourself, and remember what I said about finding another place for it to live."

Mr. McCurdy rose from his seat and walked over to the Captain. They shook hands and the Captain left. Mr. McCurdy turned back to me. His face was long and thoughtful.

"What he said is probably right. Maybe I have to think of somewhere else for Buddha to live."

"You just have to guard him, make sure that they don't let him out again," I said.

"It's like the Captain said, there isn't any way to be there all the time. Heck, I'm so tuckered out now I think I need to take a nap."

"If you took a nap, do you think that you could stay up for one more night?" I asked.

"One more night?"

"Yes."

Mr. McCurdy looked at me and smiled. "Sarah, do you have a plan?"

I smiled and nodded. "Do you want me to tell you what I have in mind?"

"Nope. If you think it'll work, Sarah, that's good enough for me."

✧

I stayed around at Mr. McCurdy's farm for the rest of the morning and afternoon. I watched the animals while he went to town to get some things we'd need and then let him have a short nap. At first he told me he didn't need a nap, but I told him it was important he was wide awake tonight and he finally agreed.

Afterward Mr. McCurdy dropped me off at my place. I walked up the driveway and went into the house. Supper was waiting for me on the table when I got in. My mother was polite and friendly, but she was definitely cold. She acted like nothing that happened had happened. She didn't even ask me where I'd been all day. I looked up from my food a couple of times and saw her looking at me and then she'd quickly look away or make small talk. I noticed that she pushed her food around the plate but didn't eat. I wanted to say something, to try and make up, but I knew there wasn't any point. Nicholas tried to kid around a couple of times, but his jokes fell flat and nobody laughed.

I think everybody felt relieved when I excused myself. First I had to make a phone call. The call went well. It was the first thing that had gone well for as long as I could remember. I wasn't sleepy but I knew I had to at least close my eyes and get some rest before the plan was put into action.

Chapter 9

I moved quietly across the darkened bedroom. There was light
from the full moon, enough light to see by, flowing in through
the window. With each step the floor creaked and groaned.
It really didn't matter. No one would suspect anything anyway.
Nicholas was peacefully sleeping, in his bed, and I moved
beside him. I looked down. His eyes were closed, his chest
gently rose up and down, and there was a soft whistling
sound as he breathed in and out through his nose. I had to
smile. I kneeled down and placed my hands tightly over his
mouth. His eyes popped open in shock and I almost broke
into a giggle as he struggled and gasped. My hands held firm
until he woke up enough not to cry out. I loosened my grip.

"SAR..." he started to shout and I choked him off again.

"Ssshhhhhhh," I whispered and released my grip.

"Sarah, what are you doing?" he whispered.

"I'm going out. Want to come?"

"What?"

"Which word didn't you understand? They were all small."
It felt good to be the one with the snappy answers. "I'll try to

speak slower. I...go...out...you...want...come?"

"Where?" he whispered.

"I'll explain everything, but not now and not here. Mom's sleeping in the next room and I don't want to wake her. Are you coming?"

"I guess I am."

"Good, come on."

Nicholas slid out of his bed. He was already dressed in his jeans and T-shirt. No matter how many times Mom threatened him he still wore his clothes to bed. While he bent down to put on his shoes I grabbed a couple of extra pillows out of the cupboard.

"What are you doing?" he asked.

"Watch." I took the pillows and laid them lengthwise in his bed, and covered them with his blanket. "There, unless mom comes right in she'll never know you're gone."

"Smart," he said, nodding his head.

I started out of the room, the floor signaling my advance.

"Stop," Nicholas whispered, grabbing my hand. "Let me lead. Try to put your feet where I put mine."

He moved in front of me and I watched as he took a few steps. The floor didn't answer him back as he walked. I tried to follow in his footsteps and was pleasantly surprised by the results. In watching him I noticed how he was walking on the very sides, almost clinging to the walls. We moved down the steps silently, with the exception of a few squeaks. We pushed through the door into the kitchen.

"Okay, Sarah, where are we going?"

"For a walk to Mr. McCurdy's house."

"Sarah, it's..." he turned around and looked at the clock

on the wall over the sink, "...after eleven-thirty. Why are we going to Mr. McCurdy's?"

"Because that's where the hunting is."

"What do you mean, hunting?" he asked. There was real concern in his voice.

"Hunting. Big game hunting."

"You don't mean that Buddha got away again!" Nicholas said with alarm.

"No, Buddha's okay and we're going to make sure he stays that way. Go and get the flashlights out of the basement."

As Nicholas ran to get the flashlights I went into the dining room and opened up the closet. I rummaged around in the back until I found what I was looking for. I held it carefully, in both hands, and headed back into the kitchen.

"SARAH!" Nicholas said in shock.

"SSSSHHH!"

"Yeah, but...the gun...what are you doing with Nana's gun?"

"We may need it. Did you get the flashlights?"

"Yeah they're right there," he said, motioning to the table, "but why do we need a gun?"

"We just might. It's not loaded. You know Mom wouldn't keep a loaded gun in the house. It's just a scare tactic. Does the gun make you nervous?"

"No! I'm not nervous about the gun, but *you're* making me nervous, really nervous," my brother said.

"Well, if you're nervous why don't you just go back to bed. I'll go by myself." I tried to sound confident but the thought of travelling across the fields by myself in the dead of night filled me with dread.

"No. I've got to go along. Somebody has to make sure you

don't get into trouble," Nicholas said.

"You watching out for me!" I said in shock. "That'll be a first! If you're coming hurry, we haven't got much time."

I opened the back door. I turned around and Nicholas was right on my heels. He barged by me to get out the door first. I pulled it closed quietly. Turning around I saw a beam of light leading away from the house. I reached over and grabbed the flashlight from Nicholas, turning it off abruptly.

"What's the big idea?" he said angrily.

"Keep the flashlight off."

"Why did we bring them if we aren't supposed to use them?"

"We'll turn them on, but later. We have to wait until we're out of sight of the house. I don't want to spook Mom."

I walked toward the field.

"Where are you going?" he asked.

"Weren't you listening to anything I said? We're going to Mr. McCurdy's."

"But shouldn't we go along the road?"

"This is a short cut...remember short cuts?"

"But it's night, shouldn't we go along the road?"

"We can't chance it. We don't want them to see us."

"Don't want who to see us?"

"I don't know exactly, but I don't want any of them to see us," I answered.

"Sarah...I think I liked you better when you were boring."

I had to smile. "Come on."

We circled around the house and started across the field. It was difficult enough during the day to find the way, but at night I was afraid it would be impossible. Nicholas grumbled and made snarky little comments as he trailed along behind me. Looking back I could no longer see the house. I switched on my light and my brother quickly followed suit. The two beams stretched out ahead of us, bobbing slightly up and down as we walked. With relief I saw the stone fence and knew we were half way there.

"Here, take this," I said. I handed Nicholas the shotgun while I climbed up and over the fence. Coming down on the other side I reached back over and took the gun from him. He scampered over after me. Up ahead I could see the stand of tall trees I'd noticed during my first trip. I aimed off to the side, exactly as I had earlier. Nicholas continued to talk, mostly just to himself, with an occasional question thrown at me. I just ignored him.

Looking up ahead I saw the outline of the barn, backlit by the moon, which was suddenly free from the clouds that had partially covered it. I clicked off my flashlight.

"Turn it off," I instructed Nicholas.

"Why?"

"I told you. We don't want any of them to see us," I cautioned.

"Any of...forget I asked," he said, shaking his head, as he switched it off.

Passing by the side of the barn, Nicholas picked up his pace until he was walking slightly in front of me. I slowed down and then stopped at the stable door. Nicholas kept on walking. I stood there, the smile growing on my face, as I watched him continue to move. About thirty or so paces along he turned to speak to me and then jumped in shock when he realized I wasn't there. He looked up and, although

I couldn't make out his face in the light from the moon, I knew it would be a combination of fear, shock and relief. Good!

I motioned for him to come back. He started to run, but before he could reach me I ducked into the stable door. Nicholas came running in after me, almost knocking me over as he bounded in through the door.

"Sarah! What are you doing?"

I didn't answer. I just walked farther into the stable. I looked around into the darkness.

"Mr. McCurdy!" I called out. I listened for an answer. "Mr. McCurdy!" I called out again, this time much louder.

I heard a rustling sound. "Mr. McCurdy!"

"Come on, Sarah, he's not here. Let's go up to the house," my brother said, tugging on my arm.

I pulled away. "He's here." I walked over to Buddha's pen. I couldn't see him at first and I feared we'd gotten here too late. Then I saw the flash of his golden eyes and a sense of relief washed over me.

"Hi, Buddha, boy. How are you doing?"

Buddha rose from the spot at the back of the cage. He moved to the front of the pen and rubbed himself against the bars. I backed off slightly. Even through the bars he made me nervous.

"Hello, Sarah," came a voice from the darkness. I turned around and saw Mr. McCurdy, carrying his gun, along with Calvin, moving out of the darkness. "Sorry I couldn't say anything sooner. I had to make sure it was you and not those darn teenagers."

"That's okay."

"Sarah, what have you got there?" Mr. McCurdy questioned, pointing at the shotgun I had cradled in my arms.

"It's okay, it's not loaded. I just thought it might come in handy to scare people."

"It's working," Nicholas said as he moved to where we stood, "because she already has me scared."

"Wonderful, you brought Nicholas along! We can use the extra set of eyes and ears," Mr. McCurdy said.

"Can somebody tell me what I'm looking and listening for?"

"I'll explain it all but first we better hide." I looked at my watch. "It's just past midnight. I don't think it'll be too long now. Where do you want us to go?"

"You and Nicholas go over there, in the far corner. Keep your eyes peeled on that door. Calvin and I will watch the upper level."

I nodded in agreement and we started for our positions.

"Sarah," Mr. McCurdy called out.

"Yes?"

"Leave the shotgun with me. It'll make the waiting a whole heap easier," he said quietly.

"But it's not even loaded," I said as I walked back and handed him the gun.

"Thank you. Now go and make yourselves comfy."

Lying there in the dark gave me time to think. It wasn't possible that it had been just over five days since we'd first met Mr. McCurdy. I shifted my weight and scratched. Little bits of straw kept getting in under my clothes. Beside me, mostly covered in straw, Nicholas was, unbelievably, asleep. I'd answered all his questions after we first settled in and then he just drifted off. Only my brother could manage that. A couple of times I'd started to have that warm 'sleepy' feeling start to seep up from my feet, into my body and into my head. Once I nodded off and my head jerked up when I realized what was happening.

Lying there, motionless and silent, I became aware of a soft rustling sound. In the darkness I couldn't tell how close it was or even what direction it was coming from. Maybe it was just Mr. McCurdy or even Calvin, shifting around above my head.

Then, I remembered who else lived in the barn; Brent the python. And I was lying right in the pile of straw where I'd seen him that first time I'd been in the barn. I heard the rustling again, much louder this time. I could just picture that snake slithering along the floor, pushing the straw out of the way, as he moved towards me. I reached out and gave my brother a little shove.

"Nicholas, wake up," I whispered. He didn't move a muscle. "Nicho...." And then I froze.

Looking across the stable I saw a soft gray outline of a figure move across the barn. Then another and another and another. I could hear the low buzz of conversation floating across the still air. The first few figures moved forward and others, two or maybe three, came in behind them. I wanted to wake up Nicholas, but I couldn't risk him gasping or jumping up and giving us away.

They moved toward Buddha's cage. I could see eight of

them as they fanned out. I could make out individual voices, a couple of them female, giggling and laughing. Buddha had moved to the back of his pen. He was crouched down on the straw, his eyes glowing brightly with anger.

All at once the center of the stable, the part where they stood, became flooded with blinding light from the spotlights Mr. McCurdy had installed earlier in the day. I shielded my eyes with my hand and Nicholas sat up like he was loaded with a spring.

"Everyone stay put or else!" Mr. McCurdy's voice thundered.

I looked up and the teenagers stood there, looks of shock and fear plastered on their faces. Two broke for the stable door and were lost in the darkness. They were getting away! Then, just a few seconds later they came back into view, walking backwards, immediately followed by Mr. McCurdy, his gun trained on them.

I caught sight of movement, just outside the line of light, moving down the stairs into the stable. It was Calvin. He came into the light, one arm on the floor, the other holding my shotgun.

"All of you. Sit down, we're going to have a little chat," Mr. McCurdy ordered.

"On the floor?" questioned a female voice.

"Oh, no!" I said quietly to myself. Although her back was to me there was no mistaking that voice. It was Erin.

"Yep, right there on the floor! Do what I'm saying! Now! My ape has an itchy trigger finger!"

Wordlessly they all plopped onto the straw littered floor. They were sitting almost on top of each other, huddled together out of fear. Mr. McCurdy walked slowly toward them.

"What do you have there?" he asked one of the boys, poking him with the end of the rifle. "Looks like a hacksaw to me. You expecting you might need one of those here tonight?"

There was no answer.

"Are you the one who let my baby go the other night?" he asked.

"I, I..." the boy stuttered.

"What's wrong? The cat got your tongue? Hey that gives me an idea. Maybe the cat would like more than just your tongue."

There was a collective gasp.

"Any of you know how much a tiger eats? About one hundred and ten pounds at one meal. Just tears it up and swallows it in big chunks. How much do you weigh, boy?" he asked.

"I, I...."

"Get up!" Mr. McCurdy ordered. The kid remained motionless. "Get up, now!" Mr. McCurdy ordered, even louder, and poked the kid with the barrel of the gun. The boy popped up.

"Come on, we're going to feed the tiger, you and me...but mostly you," Mr. McCurdy laughed sinisterly. "You don't look too happy. Don't you want to feed the tiger?"

"No, no , I don't," the boy sputtered.

"In that case, you don't have to, sit back down," Mr. McCurdy said.

"What?" the boy questioned.

"Sit down," Mr. McCurdy said, "and do it now before I change my mind!"

The boy practically collapsed into a heap on the floor.

"SARAH!" Mr. McCurdy called. "Come on over here."

What was he doing? Why did he want me to come? This wasn't part of our plan. My first reaction was total shock, but I knew I had to move anyway. I pulled myself up from the straw. My legs were numb and I stumbled slightly, regaining my balance as I moved forward. I brushed away the bits of straw clinging to my clothes. I shielded my eyes as I stepped out of the darkness and into the circle of light.

"Sarah!" I heard Erin gasp.

"Hi, Erin."

"He got you too," she said with concern in her voice.

"No talking!" Mr. McCurdy barked and Erin was silenced. "Get on over here Sarah. You're big enough to feed a tiger."

"But, I, I..." I mumbled.

Why hadn't he called for Nick, he was the one who always offered Buddha a handful of food. I always thought how easy it would be for Buddha to take off a couple of fingers along with the meat.

Mr. McCurdy leaned close. "Don't worry, Sarah, just do it," he whispered.

I still hesitated.

"Quit lolligagging, Sarah, and get on over here," Mr. McCurdy barked.

As I moved forward I was aware that every single eye was riveted on me. My legs were still a little rubbery and I was afraid I might trip.

"The rest of you get up close to the bars. I want you to get a good show," Mr. McCurdy ordered.

In stunned silence the group, five boys and three girls,

rose and spread out in front of the cage. Mr. McCurdy moved to the pen door. He reached into his pocket and pulled out a key. He leaned the gun against the bars while he unlocked, and then removed, the thick chain which replaced the one cut off the other night. Buddha rubbed right against the bars of the door. His weight pushed it slightly outward. Mr. McCurdy pulled the latch up and slipped the bolt out of the clasp.

"Okay, Sarah, into the cage, and take this." He reached into the outside pocket of his jacket and pulled something out. It was a pork chop.

"Into the cage?" I said in astonishment.

"That's what I said."

I swallowed hard, took the chunk of meat and stepped over to the door. Mr. McCurdy eased open the door slightly to allow me to squeeze through.

"Slide in, and remember, don't turn your back on him."

"I'll remember."

Buddha was right against the door. He was trying to squeeze out of the same small gap that I was trying to push in through. I held the pork chop in front of me, using it almost like a small shield.

"Hungry, Buddha?" I asked in a quavering voice, waving the piece of meat in front of his nose. He 'puffed' and then opened his mouth slightly. His tongue flicked out and he licked the pork chop.

"Toss it in and I'll give you another one," Mr. McCurdy ordered.

I threw the meat over Buddha's head and into the far side of the pen. It bounced off the back wall and landed on the floor. Buddha followed its flight with his eyes and then in one bounce he leapt across the width of the pen, 'pouncing' on the meat. As he jumped I slipped in through the opening and Mr. McCurdy closed and latched the door securely.

I was alone in a cage with an eight hundred pound tiger, in a barn, in the middle of the night. Buddha turned and looked at me. The pork chop was gone. I remembered what Mr. McCurdy said about how tigers don't chew their food. They just eat big chunks, bones and all.

"Here, Sarah, feed him this," Mr. McCurdy said.

I turned, expecting him to pass me another pork chop. Instead he was holding a chicken, a whole dead chicken, complete with feathers and feet and head and beak. He pushed it through the bars and held it out for me. I looked at him in shock, not moving.

"Take the chicken, and turn back around and watch Buddha!" he thundered.

I grabbed the bird. As I turned back around the chicken swung out in front of me, almost hitting Buddha squarely in the face as he had bounded toward me.

"Talk to him, Sarah," Mr. McCurdy said. "Talk to him."

"Ahh, hi Buddha. Are you still hungry? Do you want a chicken?"

Buddha took a few more steps and then stopped and sat down. He reached out an enormous tawny paw and tapped the chicken, causing it to swing. As it swung, back and forth in my hand, Buddha moved his head from side to side, almost like he was hypnotized by the motion. I lifted it up and tossed the bird into the air, aiming it for the far side of the pen. Like lightning, Buddha stretched up with one of his paws and batted the bird, mid-flight, directing it right into his mouth. I heard his mouth close with a sickening crunch. He looked at me with most of the chicken in his mouth. Only the feet and head dangled out of opposite sides. It looked like Buddha was smiling. He lazily strolled into the back corner of the cage. He flopped to the floor and then spit out the chicken. He grabbed it between his paws, and using his mouth, began to pluck the feathers off the bird.

"What's he doing?" I asked in amazement.

"Getting rid of the feathers. He likes chicken, but he doesn't like to eat feathers. Why don't you come on out of the cage now, Sarah."

I backed away, keeping my eyes on Buddha. The door opened and I squeezed out. I had been in the cage with the tiger, by myself, and lived to tell about it. It felt good, no, make that great, to have done it.

I looked up at the faces of the kids who surrounded me. Each had the same stunned look of total disbelief.

"Okay, kids, we have to come to some deal before you leave here tonight."

"You mean we can leave?" Erin questioned. I had to give her credit. She was the only one of this group who had actually managed to put two words together.

"Of course you can leave, right after we talk. What did you think I was going to do, kill you and feed you to my tiger?" Mr. McCurdy chuckled.

"I knew that's what they thought, judging by their looks," Nicholas piped in. Sometime while I was in the cage he'd come out of the darkness and was standing among the teenagers.

"That won't be happening, at least not tonight. What

could happen is I could call the police and have all of you arrested and charged , especially you," he said pointing to the boy who'd been holding the hacksaw. "Or we can make a deal."

"My Mom'll kill me if the police bring me home," Erin said.

"Please don't call the police. I promise that we'll never come back again," the boy pleaded and the rest nodded their heads frantically in agreement.

"No deal!" Mr. McCurdy stated loudly, and all the heads stopped moving in mid-nod. "The deal is this, take it or leave it. I'm not calling the police and you're all welcome to come back to my farm, but you have to come back as friends, just like Sarah and Nicholas. Come back to see my animals and not to hurt them."

They all looked even more stunned. Finally Erin spoke.

"You mean you want us to come back?"

"Yep, just not in the middle of the night. And, you can bring back other friends as long as they promise to respect my rules and my animals. Is it a deal?"

"We're welcome back?" questioned the boy.

Mr. McCurdy nodded.

"And we're free to leave now?" asked another.

"Yep."

"And you're not going to call the police?" Erin asked.

"No police..." Mr. McCurdy started to answer.

"Everybody freeze! This is the police!"

Chapter 10

Spinning around I saw two figures move forward out of the darkness and into the light. One of them was Officer Sinopoli.

"Okay, what's going on here?" questioned Sinopoli loudly. "These are the kids that let out your tiger, aren't they Mr. McCurdy?"

"I thought you weren't going to call the police," Erin said quietly to Mr. McCurdy.

"I didn't."

"Are these the kids, Mr. McCurdy?" Sinopoli asked.

Mr. McCurdy turned to the kids, all lined up, and looked at them slowly. His gaze passed from one to the other. He turned back to Sinopoli.

"Nope, these folks are my guests and since it's getting late, I better get them home now."

Two or three of the kids broke into smiles while a couple more looked relieved and the rest just continued to look confused. The two officers came forward until they stood in the circle of light. They looked at the teenagers who looked down at the ground.

"I know you," the other officer said, pointing at one of the boys who looked up and gave a feeble smile. "And you, and you..." he continued, pointing at two others.

"What are you kids doing here?" Officer Sinopoli asked.

"They're my..." Mr. McCurdy started to say.

"I asked them," Sinopoli interrupted sharply. "Somebody tell me what's happening here or I'm running you all down to the station."

"I already told you...."

"You were already told to shut up!" the other officer thundered.

Mr. McCurdy opened his mouth to respond, but before he could I jumped in. "We're guests! We were invited to come over and see the animals."

"In the middle of the night?" the officer asked. His tone of voice left little doubt he knew I was lying.

"Best time to see them. Don't you know that tigers are nocturnal?" I explained.

"Nocturnal?" Sinopoli asked.

"It means they're awake at night."

Sinopoli shook his head in disgust and walked over to one of the girls. "You're Michelle Hartley, aren't you?"

She nodded in agreement, looking very embarrassed.

"Do your mother and father know where you are?" Sinopoli asked.

"Sort of," she answered.

"What do you mean, 'sort of'?"

She looked over at Erin. "Well...they know I'm with Erin...sleeping over at her house."

"Hey, Frank, look at this," the other officer said. He bent

down and picked up the hacksaw which had been lying on the straw littered floor.

Sinopoli walked over and took it in his hands and turned to Mr. McCurdy. "A hacksaw, the kind that would cut through a heavy chain to free a tiger."

Mr. McCurdy didn't answer. He was still furious at being told to 'shut up'.

"Were your 'guests' planning on helping you with a little renovation work?" Sinopoli asked.

"I never ask my guests to work," Mr. McCurdy replied.

"Guests? Come on Mr. McCurdy, don't fool around. These are the kids that let your tiger loose. Let me do my job and arrest them."

"You're not going to be arresting my guests," Mr. McCurdy responded.

"Don't you want to protect your animals? If you don't let me arrest them, there's nothing to stop them from coming back again."

"I *am* protecting my animals, and I hope they do come back again. Now if you have no more business here I better help my friends get home," Mr. McCurdy said.

"I do have other business. The business that brought me here. Okay, Sarah, come along with me," Sinopoli said, pointing at me. "And, you too Nicholas," he said gesturing to my brother.

"We're guests. Why do we have to go anywhere?" Nicholas questioned as he stepped forward.

"Because your mother's telling you to," came a voice, my mother's voice, out of the darkness.

Nicholas and I both looked up in shock as a shadowy figure walked towards us and then into the light.

"Mrs. Fraser, I asked you to wait in the cruiser," the other officer said.

"I couldn't do that, not with my children missing." She turned her gaze onto me and my brother. "Sarah, Nicholas, both of you, right now, into the police car. We'll talk when we get home."

"Don't be mad at them Mrs. Fraser," Mr. McCurdy said, stepping forward. He extended his hand to shake. "I'd like to introduce myself. I'm your neighbor, Angus McCurdy."

She glared at him with a look I'd only seen once before, when my father walked out.

"I know perfectly well who you are and I will be angry if I want to be, Mr. McCurdy. As for you, you have more important things to worry about. Things like criminal charges for child endangerment or kidnapping or...."

"He didn't kidnap us," I snapped. "We came over here on our own!"

"I'm not talking to you right now, Sarah. Do as I've told you and take your brother and get to the police car, right now!"

"But..." I started to object.

"Do what your mom tells you to do, Sarah," Mr. McCurdy interrupted.

"But it's not...."

"Come on, Sarah, let's not make it even worse. Go on," he said quietly.

I looked at him, then at Nicholas and finally at my mother. I took my brother by the hand and we started to walk to the door. Over my shoulder I heard Mr. McCurdy say one more thing.

"Whatever you might think of me, Mrs. Fraser, I want you

to know I'm really sorry for the trouble I caused between you and your kids."

Walking right behind us was the other officer. Just as we were leaving the stable I caught sight of Calvin, sitting on a bale of hay in the darkness, the shotgun lying at his feet. He waved a hand but I thought it was best not to wave back in case the police officer saw him sitting there in the dark. The police car was just outside the barn. The officer opened the back door and I climbed in, followed by Nicholas. He slammed the door closed and walked back over to the stable, disappearing inside.

"Look, no handles, just like on TV," Nicholas announced in wonder.

We sat in the back of the car for another ten or fifteen minutes before Mom and the two officers reappeared. One of them opened the back door for her and she climbed in next to Nicholas. They got into the front, turned on the car, turned it around and drove down the driveway. In the darkness of the car and the countryside all I could see was the silhouettes of the two officers through the mesh screen. We turned up our driveway. Both officers got out and opened up the back doors.

"Will you be needing anything else tonight, Mrs. Fraser?" Sinopoli asked.

"No, thank you, but thanks to both of you for your help. I just want you to know this isn't like them. Honestly, they're good kids."

"That's important to remember," Sinopoli said, "and I

don't mean for us."

My mother looked at him quizzically.

"I've met your kids a few times now. I'm not happy with the way we've met but I still think they're good kids. Don't you forget it. Good night, ma'am. Good night, Sarah, good night Nicholas," he said and both officers climbed back into the car.

We watched as the car backed down the driveway. Mom walked to the house and opened the door. We trailed after her. She took a seat at the kitchen table and rested her elbows on the table and her head on her hands. We stood beside her, afraid to move, for a couple of minutes. Nicholas looked at me and mouthed the words "Should we go to bed?" I shrugged my shoulders. "Ask her," he mouthed. I shook my head no and pointed to him. He nodded in agreement.

"Mom...should we go to bed?" he asked apologetically.

She raised her head and then looked at us for a long time. Her face was sad and scared and angry all rolled into one. I felt like melting away into the floor.

"I think you better go to bed. We can talk in the morning when I'm feeling more...reasonable."

We both started to walk across the kitchen when she called out to us.

"You're never to go back to that man's property again!" she called out and we both froze.

"But he's our friend!" I protested.

"Well, I'm your mother!" she snapped and I knew instantly I should have kept my mouth shut. "I want you both to know how much you scared me tonight. How terrifying it was to find your beds empty and not know where you were. And I want you to know, especially you, Sarah, how disappointed I am, and how irresponsible and selfish and thoughtless you were. Now go to bed before I say anything else."

I stood there too stunned to move. Nicholas pulled my arm and led me through the door and up the stairs. We stopped at my bedroom door.

"Don't worry, Sarah, it'll be better tomorrow."

"Do you really think so?"

"Has to be. I can't think how it could get worse. Try to sleep," he said as he continued down the hall and into his room.

I entered my room. I started to take off my coat, but I was so tired I just flopped down on the bed. I should have gotten changed into my pajamas, but I couldn't even find the energy to pull up the covers. I stared up at the ceiling and listened for the floor boards. My body was exhausted but my mind kept humming. I could hear my mother's words going around and around and around inside my head—irresponsible... disappointed...thoughtless...selfish.

"Sarah! Wake up!"

I opened one eye to see my brother standing over me.

"Sarah, get up, you have a phone call," Nicholas said.

For just a couple of seconds as I struggled to wake up I'd forgotten just what had taken place last night. It all seemed like a dream, a bad dream.

"Who's on the phone?" I asked.

"Erin."

"Erin, our sitter?"

"You know any other Erins?"

"I wonder what she wants?"

"Go and ask her," Nicholas suggested.

"Do you think she's angry about last night? Mad about me setting them up?"

"Go and ask her."

Nicholas trailed after me into the dining room. I was relieved there was no sign of Mom. I picked up the telephone receiver which was resting on the dining room table.

"Hello," I said tentatively.

"Hi, Sarah. You and Nick okay?"

"Yeah, we're fine. What happened after we left?" I questioned.

"The police tried to convince Mr. McCurdy to have us all charged, but he wouldn't do it. Then Mr. McCurdy drove us all home. That's some cool car he has. He let me sit up front," Erin bubbled.

"That's good. I'm sorry for setting you up last night," I apologized.

"Setting me up?"

"You know, telling you that Mr. McCurdy wasn't going to be there," I said, suddenly struck by the fact that maybe she just hadn't figured it out and I should have kept my mouth shut.

"That's okay. I figured you were doing it because Mr. McCurdy's your friend. Sometimes you have to lie for your friends."

"I'm glad you understand."

"That was really something when you went into the

tiger's cage. Do you do that all the time?"

"Not all the time," I acknowledged, not wanting her to know that was the first.

"Do you think Mr. McCurdy will let me do that?"

"He might."

"Are you and your brother going over today?"

"Not today, maybe not ever," I replied.

"Not ever?"

"No, not if my mother has her way. She's really angry."

"No kidding. When I saw her face last night I wanted to crawl in with the tiger. I figured it would be safer."

I couldn't help but laugh. "Thanks, Erin. I guess I better get going. We'll see you later." I put the receiver back in the cradle.

"Well?" Nicholas asked.

"Everything's 'cool'. You talked to Mom this morning?"

"Yep, although she didn't say much."

"Where is she?"

"In the den. They faxed her some papers this morning on that big deal she's been working on. She said we should get our own breakfast, leave her alone to work and stay in the house."

I nodded my head. Maybe we wouldn't work anything out today but at least it would give her a chance to cool down a little more.

"Want to go to Mr. McCurdy's today?" Nicholas asked.

"Are you crazy?" I asked in shock.

"Naa...just kidding," he chuckled. "I wanted to see if I could get you going."

"I just wish we could call Mr. McCurdy and find out what's

happening."

"Yeah, too bad he doesn't have a phone. Are you going to make breakfast?"

"Breakfast? I'm not sure I've got an appetite."

"That's okay, I do," Nicholas said, flashing me a smile.

"Nicholas, you are just...."

"Hungry, really hungry. Some pancakes would be nice."

"You and me, together, can make pancakes," I suggested and he nodded in agreement.

We made breakfast, ate, and then cleaned up. I put on a pot of fresh coffee and had Nicholas bring Mom a cup. It was sort of a 'peace offering'. While he was doing that I went to the door to get the morning paper. Unfolding it and flipping it over I felt my heart almost stop. There, across the top of the page was a gigantic headline.

MAYOR VOWS TO REMOVE EXOTIC ANIMALS

I tore into the story. It had extensive quotes from the mayor saying how he wasn't going to jeopardize the lives of his citizens. He was making it one of his 'election promises' to rid the area of animals that 'posed a danger to public safety'.

Nicholas came back into the room. I looked up at him and my expression gave it away.

"What's wrong Sarah? We didn't make the papers again did we?"

"Not us, but Mr. McCurdy did."

"Let me see," he said, taking the paper from me.

His mouth moved silently as he went down the column. He stopped a couple of times to ask me what different words meant.

"We better not let Mom see this," Nicholas said.

"See what? What now?" Mom asked anxiously as she pushed in through the kitchen door.

"Nothing...much," I answered. "Give her the paper," I said to Nicholas.

She took it. Unlike Nicholas, she didn't move her lips as she read, but she did nod her head in agreement every few seconds.

"It makes sense. The mayor's made some very important points."

"Like what?" I questioned.

"These animals shouldn't be allowed in built up areas, around people," she noted.

"Built up? We moved here because you said you wanted to get away from all the people. Except for Mr. McCurdy we don't have another neighbor for miles."

"That's a comforting thought. If that tiger gets loose again it'll come straight for us," she said.

"You don't have to be afraid of Buddha," Nicholas said.

"Buddha?" Mom questioned.

"That's the tiger's name. Sarah wasn't afraid last night when she was in the cage."

"When she *what*?" Mom snapped.

"When she went into the cage," Nicholas repeated.

"It just gets worse and worse," she said, shaking her head. She turned to me. "Sarah, how could you do something like that?"

"I don't know."

"Well that's not surprising. You just haven't been thinking

lately. Going into a tiger's cage."

"I'm sorry," I apologized.

"Tomorrow, first thing, I'm going to call the mayor and let him know I totally support his efforts to control those animals," she said.

"The mayor can't really do anything can he? He can't make Mr. McCurdy give up his animals, can he?" I asked.

"He might be able to. It all depends on what the local bylaws say. In some places it's against the law to own exotic animals."

"But you have to understand that those aren't just animals to Mr. McCurdy. They're more like his children," I said emphatically.

"Animals are animals. You'd know that if you were raised on a farm."

I wanted to say something, to defend Mr. McCurdy, but I didn't. I just stood there and took it.

Chapter 11

It had been a long week. We were allowed out of the house but the only place we knew, or wanted to go, Mr. McCurdy's, was off limits. Nicholas suggested, a couple of times, that we just wander over during the day. It wasn't like Mom would notice. She was buried so deep in her work on that big deal she was often gone before we got up and didn't come home until we were in bed. Even when she was home her mind was someplace else. This made it uncomfortable for everybody, but it didn't seem like we had anything to talk about anyway. Even my brother seemed quiet. For years I'd wanted him to shut up once in a while, but now I wanted a little more conversation from him.

At least having Erin over to baby-sit us wasn't so bad now. She was able to keep us updated on what was happening with Mr. McCurdy. She and her friends had been over there every day. Erin told us some 'inspectors' had been up to the farm. At first Mr. McCurdy had tossed them off his property but they'd come back with the police and they checked everything out, including the stable. There was also a newspaper reporter who came to interview Mr. McCurdy. Erin said that didn't go over too well and Mr. McCurdy threatened to feed the reporter to the tiger before he tossed him off his property too.

That probably explained Wednesday's paper. The first thing that jumped out was a full color picture of Buddha, standing up on his back legs, his front paws pressed against the bars. The rest of the page had more articles, quoting the mayor, both his opponents in the upcoming election, a 'tiger expert' and some animal activists who wanted the animals returned to the wild. I thought it was stupid to think about 'returning' animals to someplace they'd never been.

From the kitchen I heard the phone ring. I kept my nose buried in my book, after all it wasn't like the phone would be for me. The noise stopped mid-ring and I figured Nicholas had answered it. I looked at my watch. It was almost five o'clock.

Mom would be home soon.

Nicholas popped in through the swinging door. "It's for you."

"Me? Is it Erin?"

"Who else? She sounded really, strange...you know, even stranger than usual."

I rushed to the phone. "Hello, Erin, is anything wrong?"

"They're coming to get the animals!"

"Who's coming?"

"The animal control people and the police," she answered.

"How do you know?"

"My mother has a friend who works at the police station," Erin answered.

"When are they coming?"

"Soon, in about an hour or two. That's why I'm calling. We're going to go out and try to stop them. All of us. We could use some help. Can you and Nicholas come?"

"I...I'd like to come, but I don't know if we can..." I stammered.

"Okay, Sarah, try and make it. It would mean a lot if you could, especially to Mr. McCurdy. I know your family just moved here but he talks as if he's known you forever. And, I think he's pretty sad about getting you and Nick in trouble with your Mom."

"We'll try," I lied. "You better get going before it's too late."

I put the phone down as Nicholas came back into the room. "Well?"

"Nothing, she just wanted to talk."

I walked into the kitchen. It was time to check on supper. I'd put in a pot roast and needed to peel potatoes and carrots to go along with it. My brother trailed behind me and started to set the table. I wasn't sure how long it would last, but all week he'd been helping, without asking.

As I finished the last potato I heard the sound of a car driving up. I looked out the window and saw Mom's car. She pulled to a stop and got out. She saw me looking at her through the window and gave me a little wave and a half-hearted smile. I was struck by how tired she looked.

"Something smells good," she said as she came in.

"Thanks," I replied, without turning around from the sink.

Mom sat down at the kitchen table, heaving her heavy briefcase on top of it with a loud thump. "Sarah, Nicholas, come on over and sit down. I have to tell you something."

The last time she sat us down like she told us we were moving. The time before that, she told us Dad was leaving. We sat down with the length of the table between us.

"I know this is going to be hard for both of you to accept, but I thought it was best that you hear it from me," she began.

I had the same feeling in my stomach as I did when I first looked over my shoulder and saw Buddha staring at me out of the darkness. Then, at least I could run away. Now there was no place to go.

"It's about Mr. McCurdy and his animals," she said.

"What about them?" Nicholas questioned.

"I want you to know it's possible that the animals may be removed...that he'll have to give them up."

"Give them up! Mr. McCurdy will never give up his animals!" Nicholas protested.

"He won't have a choice. I just wanted you to know that it could happen."

"Tonight," I said in a whisper.

"What?" Nicholas asked.

"Tonight. It's happening tonight, and you know it's happening, don't you?" I said, pointing at my mother. She looked away in a guilty manner. She *did* know.

"You know, don't you!" I accused her.

I got up from the table. "The roast will be ready at six-thirty. You should put the vegetables into the pan about an hour before that," I said as I walked over to the coat rack and grabbed my coat.

"Sarah, what are you doing?" mom asked.

"I'm going out...to a friend's place...because he needs my help," I answered.

"You're not going anywhere. Sit right back down, now!" she insisted.

"No," I answered quietly.

"What do you mean no?" she demanded

"No, as in the opposite of yes," I answered. I saw Nicholas break into a grin.

"Don't you dare talk to your mother like that!"

"My mother? My mother? You're right, I never would talk to my mother like that. My mother is somebody who used to always offer help to people who needed it! Are you my mother?" I questioned.

"What sort of ridiculous question is that?" she demanded.

"I don't know, I guess it's just the usual sort of ridiculous question," I bent down and started to lace up my shoes. "How about answering a question for me. How did you know they were taking his animals tonight?"

"I don't have to answer your questions, young lady!"

"No you don't, but my mother always answered my questions," I said as I finished lacing up my first shoe.

"Okay, fine, fine, I'll tell you! I know because the mayor and I have been talking. He sought my legal opinion."

"And what did you tell him?"

"I told him they could take the animals and hold them at least until the court says that they can't."

"So you said it was okay for them to kidnap the animals at least until a judge makes you give them back." I finished tying the second shoe and stood up to leave.

"You've made a mess of everything," I said to my Mom. "You drag us across the country and stop acting like our mother because you're too busy spending half your time being 'super lawyer' and the other half acting like some sort of over-aged, irresponsible teenager. I'm tired of being the only one who is responsible. I'm tired of having to be the parent in this family. Ever since Dad left it's been like I've been living with a stranger instead of a mother. At least he sends us a postcard sometimes. I haven't heard from my mother in over a year, and to tell you the truth, I miss her even more than I miss him. I've got to get going. I have a friend who needs my help."

I walked over to the door, opened it and stepped out.

"Young lady you come back here!" she yelled.

I turned and thought about going back. I knew how mad she was and that I'd be punished, but I also knew I'd been face to face, eyeball to eyeball with a tiger, and there wasn't much that my mother, or anybody else, could do to compare with that. She could punish me but she couldn't stop me from doing what was right. I slammed the door as hard as I could throw it. I heard a crash as it hit the door frame, followed almost instantly by the sound of smashing glass. One of the panels of glass had shattered, leaving only a few jagged shards. I took a few steps backwards and my mother's face appeared, framed by the broken pane. She wore a look of shock. I turned and walked away.

Chapter 12

I only got part way across the field when I heard Nicholas yelling after me. I stopped and waited for him to catch up.

"Did Mom let you come?" I questioned.

"Not really. A few seconds after you ran out of one door, she disappeared through the other, upstairs to her room. I left."

"I guess I really upset her. Maybe I shouldn't have said some of the things I said."

"Maybe...but I guess most of it's true. Are they really going to take the animals tonight?"

"Yes, and we're going to try to stop them from taking Buddha and Laura and Calvin away from Mr. McCurdy," I answered as we scaled the fence that divided our properties.

"Stop who?"

"The animal control people and the police and the mayor and I don't know who else."

"But Sarah, how are the two of us supposed to stop them? What are we supposed to do?"

"I don't know, but we won't be alone, we'll have help."

"Help? From who?" he questioned.

"Erin and her friends."

"Oh, great! That makes me feel much better, much better," he said, shaking his head.

Coming up to the barn I poked my head into the stable. Buddha was sitting in his pen but nobody else was anywhere to be seen. We walked up to the house. I knocked on the door. There was no answer. I heard my name being called.

"SARAH!"

I turned around and saw Erin running up the driveway, waving her arms. Nicholas and I ran to meet her.

"Fantastic, and you brought Nick too," Erin exclaimed. "Come on down this way, we're all out by the road."

As we started down the lane puffs of exhaust fumes rose into the air and an engine noise got louder as we moved closer. Rounding a curve a backhoe moved to block the way, Mr. McCurdy at the controls, with Calvin sitting beside him. The shovel was tearing away at the surface of the driveway. We walked up and peered past the backhoe. There was a sizeable hole, more than five feet deep, stretching for over twenty feet, where the driveway used to be. The dirt that had been removed to make the hole was piled on the side. Just past the mound I could see a group of teenagers, six of them, standing in front of a car.

Erin tapped me on the shoulder and motioned for us to follow after her. We scampered down the ditch and made our way around the backhoe. As we passed by, Mr. McCurdy caught sight of us. He broke into a huge grin, waved and then continued to work. Erin brought us over to her friends. They yelled out greetings and tried to talk to us, but I couldn't make out much over the noise of the engine. A stack of signs leaned against the car. One read "A MAN'S HOME IS HIS CASTLE!" The one beside it read, "A MAN'S BEST FRIEND IS HIS TIGER". Nicholas picked up a third one. It said, "LEAVE THE ANIMALS ALONE". Holding onto it by the stick attached at the bottom, my brother lifted it over his head.

The noise from the backhoe gurgled and then died away. I was just starting to turn around when a police car pulled into the driveway. It was followed by a second police car and then a van. They all squealed to a stop. The van had large lettering on the side that read "ANIMAL CONTROL." Farther away, still on the road, I saw other vehicles come to a stop. There were two more police cars, as well as an expensive looking black car and a small van. All at once the doors on all the vehicles opened and people started to move forward. A few I recognized: the Captain, the Chief and Officer Sinopoli.

Nicholas and Erin grabbed the signs and we all scrambled down the ditch and came up beside the backhoe. They handed the signs out so that everybody except me, Mr. McCurdy and Calvin had one in hand. Across the hole in the driveway the police fanned out and came to a stop. The Chief was flanked by the Captain, and a short, chubby, balding man. The Chief motioned for the officers to move forward and two started to scramble down the ditch.

"Stop right there!" Mr. McCurdy ordered.

The officers stopped in their tracks and looked back to the Captain for directions.

"These men are following a court order!" the Captain yelled back. "Let me come over and we can talk about it!"

Mr. McCurdy turned to me. "What do ya think, Sarah?

Should we let him come on over?"

"I don't think we have any choice."

He nodded. "Okay, but just you!"

The Captain motioned for the two officers to come back while he climbed down into the hole and then up the other side.

"I hope you believe me when I say I'm sorry this is happening," the Captain began, "but we have come to ensure that you allow the Animal Control people to take your animals."

"They have no right to take my animals! None of you has any right to even come on to my property!"

"I'm afraid we do." The Captain reached into his jacket pocket, produced some papers and handed them to Mr. McCurdy. "We have a court order allowing us to do both."

Mr. McCurdy dropped the papers, without looking at them, and with his heel, ground them into the dirt. "That's what I think of your papers. All I know is a man has the right to defend himself and his property."

Without warning Mr. McCurdy reached into the backhoe and pulled out my Nana's shotgun. I gasped and stepped back.

"Come on, Mr. McCurdy, let's not make this any worse," the Captain said calmly.

"I don't see how it can be any worse," Mr. McCurdy replied.

"It could get worse by you getting hurt or one of us, or one of these kids," he said, gesturing to us spread out beside him. The Captain turned from Mr. McCurdy to his officers. "Everybody take it easy! Put down your guns!" he yelled.

I looked over and was shocked to see the other police officers were no longer just standing there but were crouched down, their weapons drawn and aimed at Mr.

McCurdy. In answer to the Captain's order they lowered their guns. The Captain turned back around.

"Please put down the gun, Mr. McCurdy."

"I'm not doing anything."

Out of the corner of my eye I saw my mother push through the crowd of officers. I saw her talking with the Chief and the little man, all of them using their hands to make points. I looked over at Mr. McCurdy and the Captain and was amazed to see that they too had stopped and were staring across at my mother.

"Captain! Mrs. Fraser will be coming over to talk with Mr. McCurdy," the little man yelled.

My mother, assisted by an officer, tottered down the hole, moving precariously on her high heels.

"Who is that fella?" Mr. McCurdy asked.

"That's the Mayor," the Captain answered. "I wonder why he wants Mrs. Fraser to come over?"

"She's here to take us home," I said bitterly as she reached our side of the hole.

"Hello, I'm Ellen Fraser," she said as she offered her hand to the Captain and they shook.

"Pleased to meet you."

"Could I see the Orders you served Mr. McCurdy?" she asked.

The Captain bent down and picked up the papers. He tried to straighten them out and then brushed them off on his shirt sleeve, handing them to my mother. She looked at the first page, nodding her head slowly, and proceeded through the second and third page as we all looked on in silence.

"They all look in order," she finally proclaimed.

"Big surprise!" I snapped.

"Sarah, never take that tone with your mother," Mr. McCurdy scolded.

"That's all right," Mom said quietly. She looked at the Captain. "Can I have a moment with Mr. McCurdy, privately, and perhaps we can resolve all this peacefully."

"Certainly," the Captain observed, and walked a few steps away.

"Let's talk," my mother said to Mr. McCurdy. She walked away from where the Captain stood, stopping behind the backhoe. Mr. McCurdy walked over to her.

I followed after and I folded my arms across my chest. "Whatever you're going to say to him, I'm going to hear it too," I said defiantly.

"Fine. Maybe your brother should hear it too. Nicholas! Come!" she said, gesturing to him. He trotted over.

"Okay, what would you like to say?" Mr. McCurdy asked.

"I want to start by telling you that all the papers are in order. They have the right to come onto your property and seize the animals...."

"Yeah, thanks to your help!" I interrupted.

"Sarah! Mind your tongue. When you're rude like that it's embarrassing."

"But, I was just—"

"I know what you're doing, but it's wrong to interrupt your mom, so just listen," Mr. McCurdy said. He gently put a hand on my shoulder.

"Despite the fact they can legally take your animals, I think with a good lawyer you can get them back, but it'll take some time.".

"How much time?" Mr. McCurdy asked.

"Probably months, maybe even a year," Mom answered.

"We don't have time like that. Besides, I don't have money for a lawyer."

"I understand what you're saying. There's no choice. I'm afraid your animals have to leave the farm," she said calmly.

"There's got to be something you can do," Nicholas exclaimed.

Mom looked at Nicholas and then at me. "Sarah, Nicholas, you two have to go home right now."

"I'm not going anywhere!" I snarled. "I don't have a home!"

"Sarah," Mr. McCurdy said.

"Let me finish," Mom said, and looked directly into my eyes. "You two have to go home now and take Mr. McCurdy and his animals over to our farm."

"What?"

"The animals have to leave the farm, right now, and you have to lead them away, across the fields, to safety, on our property. The court orders only allow them to search for and seize exotic animals found on Mr. McCurdy's property. Once the animals are on our land, they're safe."

"But, but..." I stammered.

"But won't they just get more papers to take them from our property?" Nicholas asked.

"It's Friday, the courts have closed and they won't be open until Monday morning, and I'll be there as soon as the doors open to file an injunction stopping them from taking the animals away."

"But Mom, what about your big business deal? What about your firm?" I asked.

"They can survive without me for a morning. Mr. McCurdy needs a good lawyer to help him. Maybe I'd forgotten how to be a good mother but I'm still a good lawyer."

"Mom, you don't have to say...."

"Yes, I do," she interrupted. "Yes I do."

"And Mr. McCurdy can keep his animals?" Nicholas asked.

"I don't know, but at least we can try," she said, and turned to Mr. McCurdy, "if you want me to."

"I'd be much obliged if you did," Mr. McCurdy said. "What do we do now?"

"You and the kids take the animals off your property and over to our place."

"Where at our place?" I asked.

"The barn or even the house. Put something in Nicholas' room. It's so messy that even if the police had a court order to search they'd never find them," she said, and smiled. Mr. McCurdy broke into a laugh and the Captain turned around. Mr. McCurdy covered his mouth.

"You can move them, can't you?" Mom asked.

"With a little help from your kids," Mr. McCurdy answered.

"I want to stay here," I said. "Can you do it with Nicholas and Erin and maybe one of the others?"

"I can. I just need a little time," Mr. McCurdy answered.

"Get going and we'll stall as long as we can."

Mr. McCurdy handed my mother the rifle. "Be careful. It's loaded."

He called Calvin who hopped off the backhoe and came over to him. The two of them started to move up the driveway and toward the house. As Mom walked over to the Captain, I slipped over to Erin.

"Erin," I said quietly. "You and Michelle have to get up to the house."

"No way, we're staying here!" she objected.

"Mr. McCurdy needs your help. He's moving the animals."

"Wow!" Erin exclaimed.

Over her shoulder I saw the Captain turn away from my mother and look directly at us. He was now holding the rifle. I guess my mother had passed it over to him.

"Be quiet," I said softly. "Get Michelle and just go up to the house. Okay?" I walked over to hear what was going on between my mother and the Captain.

"I'm sure things can end without anybody getting hurt. I think it's a real vote of confidence that he turned over the rifle. I don't think he'll face any criminal charges for holding the rifle. He didn't actually threaten anybody," Mom said.

"I think we're both in agreement on that point. You seem to be repeating yourself." He turned to me. "Where are your friends going?"

"I think they have to go to the washroom." I was surprised by how quickly and convincingly those words popped out of my mouth.

"And Mr. McCurdy and your brother and the monkey, did they all have to use the washroom as well?"

My mother turned around and scanned the area. "I didn't even notice they weren't here. I would imagine Mr. McCurdy is getting things ready to turn over the animals. Probably he just wants a few minutes, in private, to say goodbye to his animals. We can't deny him a few minutes, but if you want I'll send Sarah up to the house to check on them?"

"I don't think that'll be necessary," the Captain said, "but

I have one question of my own."

"Well, perhaps we can answer it," my mother replied, hoping to delay things a little bit longer.

"How much time do you need?" the Captain asked.

"How much time do we need for what?"

"How much time do you need to get the animals away?" he asked.

"I don't understand," Mom said, trying to act confused.

"I'm sure you do. I've never tried to move a tiger, but I've seen it done...once before. I figure it'll take ten or fifteen minutes so why don't we just stand here and pretend to talk and argue for the next, oh, twenty-five minutes. Will that be enough time?"

They both looked at me. "That'll be long enough. Thank you," I said.

"You're welcome," the Captain replied.

"But why are you doing this? Why are you helping?" Mom asked.

"I don't know. Maybe I just like the old man or maybe I just don't like big people pushing around little people. That's why I became a cop in the first place. Why are you doing it is an even better question."

Mom chuckled and shook her head slowly. "I became a lawyer for almost the same reasons you became a police officer. I don't like seeing people pushed around."

"That's funny, up until right now you were one of the people doing the pushing," the Captain noted.

"He's right, Mom. Why are you doing this?"

"What made you change your mind?" the Captain asked.

"It was something that a very smart person said to me,"

she answered him, but looked at me.

"We better start arguing, put on a little show for every-body who's watching us. Can you threaten to sue the town?" the Captain said.

"Threaten? I was planning on doing it," she replied. "You've infringed on the rights of my client."

"Client?"

"Mr. McCurdy."

"I want you to know that this isn't the end of it," the Captain said.

"Is that a threat?" Mom questioned.

"No," I interjected, "he just wants you to know there's still a fight up ahead. They're not going to let this just end."

The Captain smiled. "That's exactly what I meant. The mayor has promised too many people and it's too close to an election, for him to back down. There's going to be a battle."

"That's okay," Mom said, "the big battle is behind me already." She turned toward me and put both hands on my shoulders. "I've got the right people on my side again," she said quietly. I could see tears forming in the corners of her eyes.

"I know this hasn't been easy, for any of us, the last year or so. I guess it's time for us to stop pulling apart and start pulling together," she said.

The Captain tipped his hat and went back across to the waiting officers.

"Thanks, Mom, this really means a lot."

"It's not a big deal. It'll be just like having an extra big house cat," she answered.

"Two," I responded. "I guess you didn't know about the cheetah."

"Cheetah?"

"Don't worry though, Laura is really gentle."

"Two, well, what difference does two make? At least it's not like it's snakes or anything. Have I ever mentioned that I'm afraid of snakes?"

"Mom," I said, putting a hand on her shoulder and thinking about how she would react when she saw Brent, "I think we better talk before we get home."

About the Author

Eric Walters is the author of eight critically acclaimed young adult novels: *Stand Your Ground* (Stoddart, 1994), *Stars* (Stoddart, 1996), *Trapped In Ice* (Penguin, 1997), *Diamonds in The Rough* (Stoddart, 1998), *Stranded* (HarperCollins, 1998), *War of The Eagles* (Orca, 1998), *The Hydrofoil Mystery* (Penguin, 1999) and *Tiger by the Tail* (Beach Holme, 1999). An elementary school teacher, father of three, crisis social worker, and soccer and basketball coach, Eric Walters lives in Mississauga, Ontario.